FADING SHADOWS

SAVAGE NORTH CHRONICLES BOOK FOUR

BY LINDSEY POGUE

AN ENDING WORLD NOVEL

Fading Shadows

A Savage North Adventure
By Lindsey Pogue

Editing by Lauren McNerney
Proofreading by Letter-Eye Editing
Cover Design by We Got You Covered Book Design

Roar Press LLC
Written and Published by Lindsey Pogue
101 W. American Canyon Road, Ste. 508-262
American Canyon, CA 94503

9781638481430

ONE
ROSS

"Once we get this loaded, I'll be good to go," Jackson said as he and I each slid a ten-gallon jug of biodiesel into the back of the Tacoma. His dark hair was pulled back behind his head, and his beard was trimmed, like he'd taken a few more moments to groom than usual this morning.

"You're stopping by the hydro plant to grab Bert and Phil on your way to the helipad, then? Or are they meeting you here?"

"Nah." Jackson distractedly combed his mustache with his bottom teeth and walked over to a stack of duffel bags. He tossed me one. "They're meeting me there. Bert wants to make sure Cory has everything he needs to run things before he leaves. And Phil went with him to make sure Bert is supervised and doesn't scare the kid away from his first lead assignment."

I grinned. "Shit, that's right. It's Cory's first time running the plant while you're all gone."

Jackson grunted as he loaded in another two diesel jugs. "Let's just say Bert's a bit unsettled about it."

"I bet he is," I muttered. Cory was a good kid, but he was clumsy." Not to mention, Bert worried something would go wrong with the hydro plant while he was away, no matter what crew we had on deck, or how powerful their Abilities were. It was admirable that he took his work seriously, but he'd been known to scare the piss out of a few recruits with the embellished horror stories that accompanied each one of his rules. It wasn't as if we would all die if the plant stopped working, but you wouldn't know that with Bert in charge.

"Then, I'm glad Phil is going to mediate. Maybe Cory will last longer than Hector did."

Jackson laughed. "Poor Hector."

"It's good for the young ones to know the responsibility of this place," I mused. It was a team effort to keep it going, now that Whitehorse housed over two hundred people. Bert was an old man who'd made it his life to keep the town running, but he wouldn't be around forever. "At any rate, the water is rushing with all the spring ice melt, so he won't have to do much. I'll be sure to check in on him from time to time though."

The clouds moved in front of the sun, which was expected on a brisk April afternoon, and a chill swept over my skin. I heaved in an ammo bin from the loading dock, curious if I shouldn't fill a smaller duffel with extra magazines and bullets, just in case. Jackson's last scavenging trip with his team, to the East, hadn't gone as smoothly as it usually did, so we'd packed weapons and provisions more generously this time.

"After hearing about that other gang altercation outside Edmonton, I'm going to get you another pack of ammo to take. Maybe some extra pistols—"

"Already thought of it," he said, nodding to the cab of the truck. "Elle wouldn't let me leave the house without extra reinforcements." The corner of Jackson's mouth lifted with amusement. It was the same contentment I saw on his face after he'd married my sister, Hannah. I'd been seeing that smirk of his more and more over the past couple of years; it looked good on him. After Hannah and Molly died, I wasn't sure he would ever be happy again. But he was, and I was glad for it.

I thought about Kelsey's plummet into insanity and her dying in my arms, then I pushed the memory away and forced myself to think about the living instead of the dead. Death was a cesspool that tended to suck me in every now and again, and it was all I could do every damn day to keep thinking about life instead.

"Beau's angry with me," Jackson said.

"Uh-oh." I chuckled and scratched the side of my face. It was always something with Beau. "What'd you do now?"

Jackson shook his head with a sigh and took a swig from his water jug. "I won't take him with me." He wiped his mustache with the back of his hand. "He hates me because of it, of course."

"Well, I don't blame you for leaving him behind." I leaned against the wheel well, feeling the cool metal through my shirt. "Whatever those gangs of kids are up to, it's nothing good. I mean, I get it—the world ends, you're ten years old, and you can move a tree with your mind, or lure a meal right toward you. But at some point, you need direction. You and I saw that all the time with the street gangs back in Anchorage, and they had parents and *normal* problems. You've got people like Nora out there, leading some of these kids around. It's crazy, scary shit. And now they're getting bored—they want more." I shook my head and thought about the fire outbreaks in the cities, caused by some of them. It was only a matter of time before the renegade youth became a bigger issue, even way out here. "I know some of them just want to be part of a pack to call family, but they're getting ballsy. They just came up on you last time, like they were fearless."

Jackson lifted his chin, eyeing me like he knew exactly what I was thinking. "So, what's your plan?"

He knew me well, and I leveled my gaze on him. Of course I had a plan. "Wall off the bridge, to start with."

"A wall?" He tilted his head back and forth as he considered it.

"We'd have to man it in order to allow those of us going between Riverdale and the prison, your place, and anywhere else outside the border, through," I admitted. "But it would give us even more control, and make us less alluring to troublemakers looking to sneak in for winter supplies, or anything else they might think we have worth stealing."

"It could work," Jackson mused, and he crossed his hands over his chest.

I shoved off the truck to head toward the few bags left to load. "It has to."

Jackson sighed. "Well, count me in. I promised to help Alex and Sophie finish their place when I get back, but it won't take long."

A month was a long time to wait to build the wall, and I wasn't sure we had that kind of time. Plus, Jackson had enough on his plate—patrolling Whitehorse with me, working on his farm, raising Beau and Thea, going on bimonthly scavenging trips—I couldn't rely on him to be a part of every project that needed doing, but I nodded all the same. "We'll talk about it when you get back."

We were far beyond the days when we could all hole up in the prison for safety, and with half of my team gone most of the time, our security measures were laughable. "As for Beau, don't worry about him," I told Jackson. "He'll get over it. I'll take him on rounds with me a few times while you're gone." I handed him one of the duffels, and we made our way back to the truck. "How long do you think you'll be gone this time, anyway? A couple weeks?" The biodiesel-powered helicopter would shave off a week's worth of driving, if not more.

"Yeah. We haven't hit up the Yellowknife area yet, and I expect we'll find plenty of supplies there."

"Yellowknife, huh?" The further out Jackson and the team went each trip, the more I wondered how long it would be before we created an installation somewhere out there.

"I left our route in Woody's office." Jackson looked at me as we nestled in the last of the bags. "Make sure he sees it when he gets back from Prince Rupert."

"Will do. They should be back soon." Kat and Woody had been gone almost a week for their quarterly check-in with Huck and his team, and it had been strangely silent without them. Despite Kat and I not getting along when she'd first arrived with JJ a few years back, we'd fallen into a groove of working together and putting up with one another.

"Aren't you glad Kat's coming home today?" Jackson slammed the tailgate shut.

My eyes narrowed on him. He and Elle had a way of asking Beau and Thea loaded questions—a parental move I usually found entertaining—and I got the feeling Jackson was using his parental voice with me now, so I hesitated to answer. "Why would I be glad?"

"Because," he drawled, "Phil and I are taking off, and she'll be coming back. You won't be alone on the safety crew." With a raised eyebrow, Jackson tried not to smile. "It wasn't supposed to be a difficult question."

"Hmm." I wasn't sure I bought that, but I let it go. "I don't know if *glad* is the word I'd use. She'll start an argument with me the moment she gets back, and then—"

"If I could get you as riled up as she does, I'd push your buttons too." He chuckled and walked over to me, shaking his head. "Just don't kill each other before I get back. We need her to help with the wall." He clamped his hand on my shoulder. "And check in on Elle for me while I'm gone, would you?"

"Of course, I will. Just get back in one piece."

"Ha, same goes for you. I noticed Meghann's had a few more concerned citizen inquiries and neighborly drop-ins than usual over the past few months. Don't let her run you ragged." Jackson winked.

I blew out an exasperated breath. "Yeah, she's uh—"

"Interested, Ross. It's called dating, you should try it sometime."

I frowned. "Don't be ridiculous."

He laughed and climbed into the truck. "Just returning the favor, brother. Don't forget how gung ho you were about me and Elle three years ago."

"Yeah, well, that's different."

Jackson stared at me, an annoyingly perceptive gleam in his eyes. "No, it's not."

"Yes, it is. You liked Elle. Meghann's nice, but . . ." I wasn't sure what she was, other than not my type. "Just get out of here, would you?" I tapped the top of the truck.

"I can see why Kat likes screwing with you so much." Jackson pulled the door shut. "It's fun."

"That's all I need—two of you on my case."

"That's what friends are for." He nodded a farewell. "I'll radio in when we get to Yellowknife."

"Sounds good. Be careful out there, brother."

Jackson waved through the open window, and with a rumble, the Tacoma started up. "See you in a few weeks!" he called, and pulled away from the loading dock, past the prison, and out the gate.

Jackson wasn't a soldier, and he couldn't burn people alive if he needed to protect himself, like Elle could, but he was a survivor and a trained trooper; he was strong and capable—you had to be, living out here. But none of that made it easier to watch him drive away. Not when so much about our lives could go wrong each day.

Even with nightly patrols around the five square miles we were using in Riverdale, the only Whitehorse neighborhood protectively nestled between the Yukon River and Gray Mountain, we were still more accessible than I was comfortable with. There were two bridges in and out that needed some sort of monitoring and defense, and the places people could hide in Whitehorse made me anxious when I allowed myself to think about it too much. No matter how much time passed, there was still so much to do.

When I realized I was still standing in the gravel drive like a sulking child, I turned for the prison—a big hulking three-story building covered in metal sheeting. I was itching to get some safety planning underway.

Bunching my long sleeves up to my elbows, I pulled the side entrance door open and heard another rumble and crunching gravel. I glanced at the open gate. Either Jackson had forgotten something, or Woody, Kat, and the others were back from Prince Rupert.

Our constant communication and trade with them were essential for keeping our growing town stocked with what few creature comforts we had, and the food and weapons we needed to sustain fifty-two adults and over 120 youth under the age of eighteen.

I recognized the sound of the Tahoe's exhaust before Woody drove through the gate. He waved and pulled up to the loading dock, bringing the Tahoe to a jolting halt. I was surprised to see that only Kat was with him.

"You just missed Jackson," I said, walking back over to greet them.

Woody pushed the driver side door open, and his rumpled, blonde-gray hair caught in the breeze. His eyes were glassy with exhaustion from nearly twenty hours on the road.

"We saw him headed into town," Woody said through a stretch.

I glanced at Kat as she flung her seatbelt off in the passenger seat. "She let you drive this time, huh? How did you manage that?" Woody wasn't the best driver in the world. He tended to steer wherever he looked, and Kat generally refused to be in the car with him at the wheel.

"She can't drive if she can't find the keys," he said with a big smile.

"True." I reached out to give Woody's hand a quick shake. "I'm actually surprised you made it back so early."

"We barely made it back at all," Kat muttered, and climbed out of the car.

I tried not to smile at her displeasure, and opened the back hatch to help unload. "It's a relief to see you're in a good mood today, Kat."

She lifted a delicate eyebrow as she pulled her hair from her bun, something she rarely did. It fell in blonde waves over her shoulders, and she massaged her head with a groan. "Either my hair tie was too tight, or I have a headache from too much whiplash." She sighed and glared at Woody.

He threw his hands up. "You shouldn't have left the keys unattended."

"They were in my bag, *my* bag, and I had to piss," she told him.

"Well, I don't know what to tell you—"

"Where are Sam and Christine?" I interjected before Kat could get too riled up. I pulled a box from the back of the Tahoe, marked Honey, and carried it to the storage container on the loading dock, empty after having loaded Jackson's truck.

"I dropped them off at their house on the way in," Woody said as he started stacking crates on the dock.

"Don't tell me all of this honey is for Thea," I joked. "Elle will kill you both."

Kat grinned as she twisted her hair back up on top of her head. "No," she said, "It's for the store. We also got some beef, some grain, and oranges shipped up from California."

"Taylor will love that," I told her. She always did nice things for Taylor, and I assumed it was because, like Kat, he'd lost his partner since surviving the Virus. Maybe they were kindred spirits or something. "He appreciates it when you get him new products for the shop."

Kat shrugged like she was indifferent to Taylor, but I wondered if that was true. She smiled a lot around him, which was unlike her. And I noticed the way he looked at her, even if I hadn't realized it until now.

As she walked over to help us unload, the side door of the prison opened with a hydraulic squeak. Stanley and Aria stepped outside.

"Ah, good ears. He *is* back," Stanley said with a smile. He looked as smart as always with his black-rimmed glasses, yellow-and-white striped bowtie, and his navy, argyle sweater.

"I told ya," Aria drawled. She sounded more like a teenager than ever. Her long brown hair hung loose around her face and bounced with each of her steps. Her freckles made her look a bit younger than she was, but her brown eyes held a lifetime of lessons and hurt already lived.

Woody's blue eyes widened with surprise and glittered with merriment when he saw them. "What the hell," he said. He tsked at Aria. "You're supposed to be in school, Smudge." Aria was tall for thirteen and came up to Woody's armpit as she gave him a side hug. Smudge was his nickname for her because Aria was such a tomboy and was always dirty. A lot had changed in a few years, though, and like Thea, she was getting older. Both of them would be causing boy trouble soon enough, and I didn't envy any of the pseudo-dads in the slightest.

"Aria went to school this morning," Stanley explained, "but Sophie sent her home at lunch, since she knew there would be family matters to attend to." He clasped Woody on the shoulder with a warm smile.

"We've got the rest of this, Woody," I told him, and waved him away. "Go on, I'll finish up out here."

"I think I'll take you up on that," he said, and with his arm around Aria, the three of them walked back toward the prison. I watched with a strange mixture of relief, happiness, and sadness. They'd found their niche again. All of them had been lost at the beginning, but now they had their people, a family—two crazy uncles and their ward.

"When are they going to get a place of their own?" Kat asked as she lifted the crate of oranges out of the back with a huff.

"I don't know. They've mentioned it a couple times, but I guess they like it here."

"When we actually start using the prison how it's meant, they won't be able to raise her here."

I reached further into the back of the Tahoe and pulled out two metal crates. "It's not my business." Glancing down at the bottled homebrew, I grinned. "Let me guess, these are for you." I knew how much she liked Huck's ale.

"No, actually. I didn't get any for myself this time. Huck didn't have a lot, so I just brought some for Taylor's store. I figured I can wait until we go back again to get more."

"Aw, how thoughtful."

"Shut up, Ross," she grumbled.

With a smirk, I stepped past her.

"Oh, wait," Kat said, turning for the back seat. "I almost forgot the meds." She hauled out a decent-sized box and set it inside the storage container. "We'll need to decide what goes to the store and what we should keep for the hospital," she thought aloud.

"That reminds me." I leaned against the car. "What did Huck say about the serum?"

Some of the Hope Valley folks had been working on a remedy that reverted the effects of the Virus in survivors' genetic code, helping people whose Abilities were too much of a burden in their everyday lives feel a bit more normal and in control. It actually started out as a possible "repair" for the Crazies and their Ability-broken minds. Then, the focus shifted to older people who had a hard time controlling their Abilities, probably because of their age, and were an endangerment to themselves and others by no fault of their own. And it was an intriguing option to people like me, who didn't want their Abilities at all.

Kat's steely blue eyes met mine. "They're looking for volunteers to try it out," she said, hesitating. "I'm thinking about doing it."

"What? Why?" My tone was harsher than I meant it to be, but I couldn't help my shock. "Kat, you don't even know if it will work—what if you die?"

"Careful, Ross. You almost sound like you care." She smiled, but I wasn't amused.

"I'm serious. It's not like I want to be tethered to death, but even if my Ability was magically gone one day, I wouldn't be able to forget the past—not every life that's passed through me and what it's felt like; not the memories. That's assuming I survived the effects of it at all. Why would you risk being a guinea pig?"

She shook her head. "Why not?"

"I can think of a hundred reasons." No one wanted to feel people die, like I could, but manipulating electrical energy—the ability to bend it to her will if she ever cared enough to use it— didn't seem that bad; not enough to be so reckless. Especially not when she had people who cared about her, who she might risk leaving behind if her decision to experiment with something so unknown went horribly wrong.

"Well, it's not your call," she said flatly.

I crossed my arms over my chest and stared at her. Kat's Ability was a topic she often avoided, and I never pressed her because I didn't think it was my business, even if I was curious as hell, but how nonchalant she seemed about it felt too hasty, even for her. "Why won't you tell me why you hate your Ability so much?"

"Because it doesn't matter, Ross. Drop it, okay?"

I hated that I didn't have a card to play that would force her to tell me. She would laugh in my face if I pulled rank as her boss and demanded an answer. She would make some snide remark if I told her I wanted to know why it affected her so much because I cared. So, biting my tongue, I turned back for the Tahoe. Kat didn't open up about much, so I wasn't surprised she was shutting me down, but I didn't like it.

When we were finished unloading, Kat grabbed her pack from the back, her slender, muscle-hewn arms straining, then she dropped it to the side with a thud.

"What do you have in there, bricks?" I joked, trying to lighten the mood a little. The last thing I wanted was us ignoring one another so soon after she got home.

"Weapons. My radio—" She shrugged. "Stuff." Kat wasn't a delicate flower, I'd give her that. "Also, I need a ride to the farm before you go on patrol this afternoon, so I can check on Puck and help Elle with dinner."

"I'm not going to dinner tonight," I told her, handing her the last of the bags before closing the back. "Just take the Tahoe. I have my truck."

"I'm riding Puck home. The Tahoe will be a wasted vehicle." She dropped her hands from her hips. "Besides, why aren't you coming to family dinner?"

"Phil and Jackson are gone, and you're going to the farm—there's no one to make the rounds."

"Um—you're the boss, Ross. You can do whatever the hell you want. Change the damn schedule, no one will care—hell, no one will even notice."

"Wow," I said, shaking my head. "I feel so validated right now."

"Sometimes the truth hurts." She hit my shoulder. "But seriously, no one will care."

With a sigh, I nodded to my truck, under the carport at the end of the loading dock. "Fine. Grab your shit."

"Perfect. I knew you were sensible."

I glared at her. "Were you this wonderful in your past life? Or am I just lucky to have you as my only deputy for the next few weeks?"

Hauling her large pack over her shoulder, Kat looked back at me with a sassy smile and winked. "You're just *that* lucky."

TWO
KAT

"Here we are," Elle sang as she stepped outside with two glasses of red wine. She handed me a glass, half full, and then clinked hers against it. "To an impromptu happy hour."

With a dip of my chin, I smiled. "Why, thank you."

Elle grinned, slid the screen shut, and took a sip from her glass before she sat on the lounge chair beside mine. I wasn't much of a wine drinker; at least, I didn't use to be. I'd always liked to hang out with the guys from my squad, drink beer, spit sunflower seeds at baseball games—and don't get me started about my competitive streak. I assumed those were real memories, but I sometimes still questioned which parts of my mind were original and which had been tampered with. My time with JJ was all I knew for certain had been *me*, and I figured that's why I'd clung to her so much. It was why I loved her, even when she hadn't loved me back.

Slowly, wine was becoming more enjoyable, though. *Very* slowly. Elle liked it, and I enjoyed Elle's company, so I tried to find things I appreciated about it—for instance, it was alcoholic and gave me a good buzz when I needed one; drinking it made me feel different from who I was before, like I was truly starting over and becoming a person I was choosing, not who I was told or programmed to be. I took a tentative sip.

Finding what I liked about wine wasn't always easy. It made my lips pucker, my tongue twitch, and felt dry going down the back of my throat.

"You don't like it," Elle observed with far too much amusement.

I swished it around in my mouth, trying to get a real taste of it, the way we'd read a person is supposed to do in a book she'd found. Then, I shook my head. "It tastes like sour jam, same as the one last time."

Elle reached for my glass, still held between my fingers, to take it away. "Excuse you," I quipped.

"I don't want you to be miserable," she said with a laugh. "I'll get some of Alex's brew from the fridge. He won't mind, and I know that's your preference anyway."

"Elle," I said, sheltering my wine glass against my chest. "In the three years you've known me, have I ever turned an alcoholic beverage away?"

Her green eyes brightened again, and she shook her head. Her dark hair brushed against her shoulders. "No, actually." She leaned back in her lounge chair.

"Well, other than my partiality to moose jerky, and my increasing fondness of children, nothing's changed. I'll drink it."

With a contented grin, Elle closed her eyes and lifted her face to the afternoon sun as it peeked through the clouds. "Suit yourself."

I settled back into the cushion and took another sip. "There are subtle hints of cherry, which I like."

"There you go, getting my hopes up again," she murmured. "I commend you for trying, though. I don't drink when Jackson is around. He says he doesn't mind my drinking, but I don't like to."

I knew Jackson wasn't much of a drinker, at least not these

days. Although I never heard the story, I got the feeling it was his vice, just like working was mine. I had no life, outside of working with Ross, to prove it.

"Is that why we're drinking at three in the afternoon, because you have the house to yourself?" I set my glass on the side table between us. "I never pegged you as much of a day drinker."

Elle's lips parted into a small, knowing smile. "Only on special occasions. And an impromptu happy hour with my best friend, after her being away, is definitely one of them." Her eyes flitted open, and she peered out at the property that stretched around us. It was much the same as it had been when they'd built it, maybe with a few more animals and an additional pasture. The greenhouse was brimming with greenery, and I wasn't sure how Elle and Jackson kept up with all of it.

"Let me guess, it's rough business without Jackson being home, huh?" Elle didn't have to answer, I knew her well enough now to know she was never whole without him. Not that she wasn't capable of being alone, because she definitely was—she could protect the homestead, run it, and mediate Beau and Thea without him just fine—but she was anxious when he was away, especially knowing how increasingly dangerous it had become during the past couple of outings. We all tended to be anxious for everyone's sake when they left: for Ross, Woody, Phil, and even old man Bert. Things in our lives felt a bit more settled, but they would never be predictable. Everything always carried a certain amount of risk.

Briefly, I wondered how much Ross still thought about his fiancé. Obviously he'd loved her, since he was going to marry her, but did he still think about her every day? Did seeing Elle and Jackson together remind him of his old life and what he'd lost?

I loved JJ with every ounce of who I was, but I felt my memory of her fading. I felt the anguish subsiding with it, and though I wanted her to be alive, I'd come to terms with her wanting to die a long time ago. But for Ross, the woman he loved was taken from him; she hadn't chosen to leave. My situation was very, very different.

That I was pondering Ross's love life at all was bizarre, but I chalked it up to the fact that, while I was gone, I'd kinda missed him glaring at me every chance he got. And his laugh too, when he forgot he was supposed to be a serious hard-ass all the time.

I cleared my throat. "Where are the kids, anyway?" If I had a watch, I would've checked it, but out here we gauged time on the ascent and descent of the sun. Batteries—save for what we needed to run machines or heavy equipment that Bert and one other citizen, Kev, could manhandle with their Abilities—were officially out-of-date.

"Sophie is bringing them home with her, but she had a couple things to do."

It was a vague answer, but I didn't pry. "Stanley took Aria out of school today, to welcome Woody home," I told her. "He was surprised, it was sort of sweet."

"Aw, that's so thoughtful of Stanley."

I leaned my head back and tried to remember my own family. I couldn't, not even in the slightest. College in Anchorage was as far back as my memories went, then I'd enlisted in the Army. I knew Herodson's programs focused on homeless and sick populations of people to use or experiment on, people who had little to lose or were already weak and pliable. I assumed I had been one of the two, and I tried to decide whether knowing that made me sad, or if I should be grateful that I didn't remember at all.

Whatever Aria's life with Nora was before the guys had taken her in, she had people who loved her and cared about her now. "They're a funny family, aren't they? Cute, but funny."

Elle chuckled softly. "For the first few months Aria lived with them, I waited for Woody or Stanley to tell me they couldn't handle a little girl, but they never did."

"I saw Woody mending her scraped knee the other day," I told her. "It was pretty damn cute."

With an amused sigh, Elle took another sip from her glass, then licked her lips. "That's one thing Stanley still struggles with, and I can't help but laugh."

"Blood?"

"Blood, tears, snot—he's too OCD for it. But Woody doesn't mind taking the lead on things like that, he's got the protective thing down. And Stanley . . . he's the nurturer. Aria is very lucky to have them."

We sat in easy silence for only a second before hammering echoed through the cool afternoon. I peered into the trees. "Is that Alex?"

Elle nodded. "He's been working on that cabin for weeks. Jackson and some of the guys from town have been helping. He's trying to get it finished before summer since he hates working in the heat." Her demeanor changed slightly as she stared into the woods, and her openness faded. "It will be a good place for them, I think."

"I see, and how do you feel about them moving out?" Alex and Sophie had been a constant part of her life for the past five years. Their household of six would soon only be four.

With a small shrug, Elle shook her head. "I want them to be happy and have a life away from us. It's the whole point of being here—to start over. I'm happy for them. I hope they get everything they want."

There was a strange longing in Elle's voice that was a bit more saddened than I'd expected. "But?"

"Oh, nothing." She forced a smile. "I'll miss them, that's all. And"—she held up her hand—"before you say it, yes, I know they will be just across the river. . . but still."

"I wasn't going to say anything," I promised affably, and I took another sip of my wine. The taste of it grew on me with each swallow.

Elle sat up and turned to face me. "Okay, so I have a question, which you're not going to like, but I'm going to ask it anyway."

I groaned and set my wine glass down. "Great. So, *that's* why you're getting me drunk."

"No—well, sort of," she admitted.

"Are you saying I'm not approachable, Elle?"

She stared silently at me in answer. At first, it was difficult to look at Elle after JJ died, but I'd since realized that they were different in so many ways, despite being twins, and being around Elle wasn't as difficult as I thought it would've been. Or maybe enough time had gone by, so that everything was just . . . easier. "Well, spit it out," I said, heaving out a breath in preparation. "Lay it on me." I took another hearty sip from my glass.

"Ross told me about the serum . . ."

Rolling my eyes, I threw one of my hands up. "Wow. When the hell did he have time to tell you that?"

"You were in the bathroom."

I growled and looked at her. "First Woody, now you and Ross. Why is everyone always conspiring against me when I'm in the bathroom?"

"First of all," Elle said, holding up her hand. "We weren't conspiring. Secondly, he's worried about you."

"Right, well," I said, turning to face her fully. "Did Ross tell you he was considering taking it too?"

"Yeah, but Kat, a lot of things sound better in theory. Do you really want to be experimented on *again?*"

I let my head fall back, and stared up at the cloudy sky as she continued.

"I mean, what's so bad about what you can do? Controlling electricity could be so helpful—it could even protect you one day. Why do you hate it so much?"

Squeezing my eyes shut, I tried not to imagine my handprints charred into JJ's chest.

"I know we don't talk about Jenny all that much, but had her choice been different—if she'd wanted to live—you could've saved her. That's a good thing. Think about what else you might be able to—"

"That's the point, Elle, isn't it? She didn't want to live anymore—from the moment I saved her life. I brought her back in Whitely, and she didn't even want me to." It wasn't that I was completely decided on taking the serum, but the idea of not feeling the electrical charge in the air when the weather was turning—knowing I'd never have to smell burnt flesh again at my own hands—would be a reprieve. Even if it was JJ's face that flashed in my mind when I thought about it, despising my Ability wasn't about her and what I'd inadvertently done to her anymore, but more the desperation and fear I never wanted to feel again. I hated being reminded of it, and I hated feeling weak; and, if I was honest, I hated feeling the lingering sting of JJ's rejection that always accompanied it, like somehow, I would never be enough—for anyone.

I forced myself to look at Elle. Her green eyes glittered with sympathy, and I hated that too.

"I don't want to talk about this," I told her. "And I can't believe Ross told you."

"Why not? He's clearly worried about you."

"I'm not sure why," I grumbled.

Elle barked a laugh—a full, hearty sound I hadn't expected—and my wine nearly sloshed over the rim as I jumped. "What the hell is so funny?"

"You. And Ross," she said, more under her breath than to me.

"What—why?"

Elle took another drink from her wine glass, peering at me over the rim.

"Stop looking at me like that. It's creeping me out."

Licking her lips with a familiar, knowing glint in her eye,

Elle lay back against the cushion again. "The two of you are just so funny."

I studied her nearly empty wine glass, rolled my eyes, and settled back into my chair. I'm not sure where Elle's mind was wandering off to, but it made me uncomfortable. "God, you're such a lightweight."

She flashed me a sideways glance. "Whatever makes you feel better."

A low chuff met my ears, and Elle and I both glanced toward the edge of the woods, down by the river. Honey Bear, otherwise known as Bear, named by Thea, poked his head out from the trees in all of his grizzly bear glory. His black, wet nose shimmered in the sunlight, no doubt looking for Beau or food as he ventured closer. He sniffed the air, chuffing again, then took a step closer.

"He's not here, Bear," Elle called without lifting her head from the lounge chair cushion. It was as if she was telling one of the neighbor kids that Beau couldn't come out to play.

Bear's furry brown head turned in our direction, and slobber dripped from his mouth. He made what sounded like a whimper before he turned back into the woods.

Elle took another sip of her wine and closed her eyes with a sigh. "It's like I live with Dr. Dolittle," she muttered, and as soon as the words rolled from her tongue, we both laughed.

I held up my wine glass. "It could be worse. You could be living with the Pied Piper or something."

She grimaced and clicked her glass to mine. "I'll drink to that."

THREE
ROSS

I broke off a piece of cornbread to mix into my chili. It was Kat's recipe, one she'd picked up from her squad leader when she lived on Joint Base Elmendorf–Richardson in Anchorage. There was just enough chili powder to give it an unexpected kick, which I appreciated.

"So," I said, glancing up from my bowl. "Any word from Del and the gang since they went home to air out the old house?" I looked around the table; first at Woody and Stanley, who sat across from each other, down by the kids; then at Alex and Sophie as they eyed one another in a private moment; and finally, to Elle and Kat. With all of us running around in different directions, family dinners seemed to be the only time we really got a full update on everything.

Elle's gaze flicked to mine, and she set her spoon down. "They're already taking full advantage of spring," she said. "Jade mentioned getting a head start on her teas this year while Took and Del were caribou hunting." Elle's eyes crinkled in the corners, and she smiled. "I think she might finally listen to you and trade some of them at the summit this autumn."

I grinned and felt a slight satisfaction in that. It was one thing for us to strive to live a life similar to what we'd been used to before the outbreak, but for a family like the Ranskins, it was different. While Del had a ranch out west before moving to Alaska, Jade and Took had lived off the land their whole lives. Them embracing electricity was a milestone in itself; and now, Jade was carving out a niche for herself in the new world we'd all been working so tirelessly for, and it made me feel an unexpected sense of pride.

"Maybe we'll turn them into city folks yet," Kat said with a smirk, and she scooped another spoonful of chili into her mouth.

"Jade said coming here is like a vacation," Elle said, and wiped the corner of her mouth with her napkin. She dropped it into her bowl. "I think the running water is what did it." She winked at Thea, whose brown eyes darted between us as she licked her lips.

"I'm just glad they are actually coming back in the winter," Beau muttered, and he glared at Aria. "Bear scared the crap out of them last time."

Aria glowered back at him. "Don't look at me. *You're* the one who keeps pushing him away and won't be his human."

"His name is Honey Bear," Thea interjected. "Not *Bear*."

"That's a stupid name," Beau grumbled.

"No, it's not," Thea countered with more sass than I'd heard in a while. Her nose scrunched and she glowered at him. "You wouldn't name him, so *I* did."

Elle sighed heavily, and she rubbed her forehead like she knew where their conversation was headed.

"He's not my bear to name," Beau said, staring accusingly at Aria.

"Well, he's not mine!"

"Yes, he is. I have the wolves—"

"God, you're so annoying," Aria huffed.

Beau rolled his eyes at her. "Whatever. He's only around because of you."

"And he only gets into trouble because of *you*—"

"Okay, you two," Woody grumbled, setting his spoon in his bowl with a clank. "That's enough. We're at the dinner table."

I looked from Woody and Stanley, to Elle, wondering if Beau and Aria would ever grow out of their blame game phase. None of us *could* send the bear away, and neither of the animal whisperers *would*. Bear wasn't dangerous, so much as acting out, like a teenager seeking attention from his divorced parents. Aria might've been his mother's human, but Coco was gone. She went away, to do whatever grizzly bears do, the moment Bear was old enough to fend for himself. Only he never really went on his own, and without a human, I had a feeling the three-hundred-pound bear cub was struggling, and as confused as Beau and Aria were.

"You could at least act like you care about him," Aria muttered under her breath, and I took a hearty gulp of iced tea. I wasn't touching their ongoing animal telepathy argument with a ten-foot pole.

"It doesn't matter," Sophie said, less delicately than usual. "We have more important things to worry about than Bear. In fact, maybe having him around will be useful." Concern etched her forehead as she pushed her half-eaten bowl of chili further away.

Elle glanced from Sophie to the kids. Each of them seemed to be an inch taller every time I saw them, but they were still personalities apart.

Deftly, Stanley lured them into a conversation about Bear's wild nature and how pushing boundaries was what children did, which in essence was what Bear was.

"How do you mean, Soph?" Elle asked, and I had a feeling I knew what Sophie was going to say before she continued.

"Whitehorse won't be much of a vacation destination if we can't figure out how to keep everyone safe." Alex scooted her bowl toward himself to finish what remained, and she sat back in her chair. "What did you find out about Edmonton?" she asked, looking from Woody to Kat. "That ambush Jackson and the team had to deal with last time hasn't been the only one, has it." It wasn't really a question, which meant she'd been talking to someone.

Kat and I looked at each other. "Christine," we both muttered at the same time. As a part of the city council, she was privy to information we didn't openly share with the entire town, not until we'd thought it through a little bit more. But Christine had a hard time keeping her mouth shut, which made her the towns-people's favorite person when they couldn't put their curious minds to rest.

Tucking her loose, strawberry blonde hair behind her ear, Sophie crossed her arms on the table, waiting for an answer.

Woody ensured that Aria, Beau, and Thea were lost in their own conversation before he answered. "The groups, or gangs, if you want to call them that," he said quietly, "aren't isolated incidents, no. There's been word of a few of them in Washington, and the Midwest too, from what Huck's been told. There are rumors of violence, and they've left burned towns in their wake, almost like they want to prove a point."

"Or," I added, "it's more malicious, and they want to make it more difficult for survivors on the move to find shelter."

"Well, it's no wonder these teenagers are getting so comfort-able," Elle said, then took a sip of her water. "There are hundreds of miles of nothing so they can do whatever they want and go unchecked."

"It's their Abilities I'm worried about," Sophie said. "Many of them are much stronger than us." It was part of the genetic makeup of the younger generation. They grew up with the Virus in their blood; they wielded it better and more freely than those of us whose bodies had passed maturation before the outbreak.

"Huck wants to establish a patrol of some sort," Kat added,

and while her words were meant to put Sophie at ease, I hoped that Kat realized it was unrealistic.

"There are thousands of miles of wilderness between what refuges are established. I'm not sure how possible that will be," Sophie told her, echoing my very thoughts. Some Abilities could help us cover that amount of space more easily, but we had a city and people to protect, and the woods were more like no-man's-land, surrounding us in all directions from here to Hartley Bay, and even up through Anchorage.

"I say we block the bridges," I told them. "We focus on home, first. Prince Rupert could manage that easily enough—there's only the one bridge in and out. Same with us. Riverdale has the one road in and out, and a wall or barricade would be a deterrent."

"What about those of us outside of Riverdale? It's only a neighborhood in the grand scheme of things," Alex said. "What about the rest of Whitehorse—the hydro plant, the homestead here, even the prison? They wouldn't be protected." He wrapped his arm around Sophie's shoulder, and she leaned into him. I wasn't sure if Elle noticed, but I got the feeling there was something more than teen gangs that creased Sophie's brow with worry.

"It was a risk Jackson and I knew we'd be taking by settling out here," Elle said, her voice low and thoughtful. "But Ross is right—Riverdale would be easy enough to close off, and these teens seem to be going for the communities that have easy access."

"It's an option," Kat agreed. "But only until we outgrow Riverdale."

"We've got some time for that yet," I told them, and took another swig of my iced tea. "Either way, something needs to be done. I've already talked to Jackson about it."

There was a lot I missed about my life before the Virus, like falling asleep with Kelsey beside me, and the smell of her skin, fresh out of the shower. I missed her gentle sneezes when she vacuumed the house, which happened a lot because she was more obsessive-compulsive than she ever would've admitted. I missed the structure of the every day and knowing what to expect, like football Sunday at Jackson's house, and gorging myself on Hannah's famous lasagna. I missed so much of my old life, but not the late-night patrols on desolate, backcountry roads. Not the sound of my radio clicking on for a final call before I ended my shift, wondering if it might be my last. Over the past few years, we'd only had a few run-ins with Crazies during scavenging trips. We were vigilant and prepared. I didn't want these unruly teens to ruin that.

"There's plenty we can do here to prepare for whatever comes next, before we start sending folks off to patrol the unknown." I glanced at Woody. "I'd thought this could wait until tomorrow, since you've only just returned, but we better put together a town meeting before Christine scares the shit out of everyone else with the news, if she hasn't already."

"—itchy ass."

We all paused and peered down the table at Beau.

"Whatever," Thea said, rolling her eyes at her brother. "You're lying."

Beau shrugged and threw his hands up in annoyance, but I could see the amusement creasing the corners of his eyes. "I didn't make it up. Ask Jackson when he comes home."

"Yeah, right," Thea muttered, but her gaze lingered on her brother, trying to decide if he was tricking her. At eleven, Thea was old enough to know better when it came to believing everything Beau told her, but I could tell she still found it hard not to wonder sometimes. He was her older brother, after all. When I was thirteen, I was protective of Hannah, but I enjoyed teasing her, just as much as Beau seemed to enjoy screwing with Thea.

"What's this?" Elle asked, turning in her chair to face them.

"It doesn't sound like appropriate dinner conversation." She eyed Beau sharply.

With wide, knowing eyes, Beau shrugged. "I was just repeating what Jackson said."

"Which is?"

"Thea found a hair in her chili, and Jackson said if you eat a caribou hair, you'll get an itchy ass."

Elle frowned. "First of all, that's not true." She examined the hair, wiped on Thea's napkin. "And that's a Luna-hair," Elle told her. "See . . . it's black. I bet if you stopped sneaking her in under the table, you wouldn't have that problem." She leveled her gaze on Beau again. "Stop teasing your sister."

Beau rolled his eyes.

"It was an old Yup'ik saying," Alex added. "Jackson didn't say it was true."

"Whatever," Beau muttered, and dropped his spoon into his bowl of chili. "Can I be finished?"

Elle nodded into the kitchen. "Only if you take your dirty dishes to the sink and rinse them."

Beau took his sister's empty bowl, then Aria's, and stacked them in his without being told. Then he stood and reached across the table to collect Stanley's and Elle's. Even if he liked to grumble and groan and act like the world was against him, Beau was a good kid; his heart was always in the right place. He'd wanted to go with Jackson and help, and I understood that.

I wondered if Elle and Jackson still saw Beau as the little kid he used to be, with his feet barely touching the floor when he sat at the table, or if they realized he was a young man in need of a purpose.

"Hey, Beau?" I said.

He stopped halfway to the kitchen and turned around to look at me.

"Phil's gone, and I could use some backup during my rounds tomorrow. Are you and Luna interested?"

Beau's eyes widened ever so slightly, and I could tell he really wanted to, even if he wouldn't allow himself to show it. "Can I?" he asked Elle.

A small smile tugged at her lips. "You can," she said, "but," —Beau's brow crumpled a little—"you have to do everything Ross tells you. You have to listen to him."

"I will," Beau said, his voice more eager. "I promise." He made his way into the kitchen with a little more pep in his step.

"Speaking of work," Kat said, pushing out her chair. "It's getting late. I'm going to get Puck ready to leave."

Thea jumped to her feet. "Can I help saddle him?"

"Of course," Kat said with a smirk.

"Come on, Aria, you can help too." Thea waved for Aria to follow, her single ponytail swinging, and they both hurried behind Kat, toward the door.

"Thanks for cooking tonight, Kat," Elle said.

Kat looked over her shoulder, at the empty wine bottle in the center of the dining table. "No problem." She winked, like the two of them had a secret, then she waved the girls out the sliding glass door to ready the horse.

"We'll clean up," Sophie said, and she and Alex scooted their chairs out.

"I'll get all these," I told them, and collected the water pitcher and a couple of empty glasses. Sophie and Alex cleared the leftover chili and what was left of the cornbread off the table.

Elle tucked the empty wine bottle under her arm and gathered her and Kat's empty wine glasses. If I hadn't known any better, I'd have guessed that the rosiness of Elle's cheeks was from a few glasses of wine, not the warmth of the house.

"Now that Kat's taking Puck back," she said, following me into the kitchen, "Thea wants another horse."

"Oh, so Big Red doesn't count anymore, huh?" I slid the water pitcher into the fridge.

"She wants a proper horse, one she can ride."

"Oh, a *proper* horse. Got it."

Elle chuckled and shrugged, as if dealing with the whims of preteens had become second nature. After nearly five years of all of them together, I guessed it would be.

"Come on, I'll walk you out." Elle headed for the sliding door.

"Thanks for dinner," I said, patting my stomach. "Spicy *and* delicious."

"And that was all Kat," she countered. "But of course, you're welcome. I'm glad you came. I know you're short-handed right now."

"You'll let me know what I can do, won't you, Ross?" Alex said, brushing the crumbs off the kitchen table. "With the wall?"

Even if my inclination was to say yes, I hesitated. Alex had a house to finish building, and whatever had Sophie so distracted was disconcerting too. But as Alex straightened, waiting for my answer, I nodded. "You got it." Elle was right, I was short-handed, and Alex's Ability to amplify other Abilities would cut the time it would take us to make the barricades in half. "And once the barricades are up, I'll help you finish that cabin."

"Deal." Alex glanced into the kitchen with a concerned look on his face.

"Uh, see ya, Soph," I called.

"Bye, Ross!"

I opened the sliding door for Elle, and we stepped outside.

It was dark out, but the pasture was lit up like a football stadium on game night. I glanced down at Kat and Thea as they brushed Puck at the pasture fence.

"Let's see how long it takes Thea to ask me if she can have a horse," Elle muttered and we walked toward the deck steps.

"You mean, how long before you actually get one for her? Because we both know that's going to happen." The night air was brisk, and I could barely see the pale light of dusk behind the mountains.

"Correction—*Jackson* will get it for her. I don't need another animal to take care of. That's why we gave Beauty to the Ranskins, to begin with."

I wondered if it wasn't the only reason they took Jenny's horse to the Ranskins, but also that Beauty reminded Elle of Jenny, which was too painful at times, and perhaps why Kat hadn't stopped her.

"What do you think about this business of Kat moving into town?" I asked her, knowing that, especially with the gangs on the move, Elle would feel more comfortable if Kat stayed closer.

"Oh, well, I think it's great," she said, shocking the shit out of me.

I stopped on the top step and peered down at her as she reached the bottom. "You do?"

When Elle realized I wasn't behind her, she glanced up at me. "Yes. Why wouldn't I? Kat needs her own life, just like you do, and Bert, and the Ranskins . . . and being cooped up here with me and the kids isn't going to get her out there, dating or meeting new people, and having a life."

"Dating?" I asked. Elle's eyes rounded, fixed, and studied me, and I shook my head. "I mean, that's all fine, but that's not the point. She chose the worst time to leave the farm. Her house is on the outermost part of Riverdale, and now there's the issue of these damn gangs." I glanced at Thea and Kat as Aria headed into the barn, Big Red following behind her, likely expecting some treats. Kat lugged Puck's saddle onto his back effortlessly while Thea watched, riveted.

"Kat's house is only, what, a couple of blocks from yours? I think she can manage, Ross. Besides, she needs that place if she's going to keep the horse, and you know Kat. She'd rather get around on Puck than drive."

"She won't use a patrol vehicle *because* I asked her to, there's a difference. She knows it would make me feel more comfortable," I explained. "And I can't help but think she took that house on the hill because I told her it was a bad idea, too."

"Of course, it's all just to piss you off, right?" Elle answered with a gleam in her eyes. I attributed it to the wine and the halo of light we walked through. "It's not at all because it has a little barn and pasture for Puck. Or because she likes the peace and quiet, like what we have out here. It's not because it's Kat, who barely likes people as it is. It's all because you told her not to."

"You know what I mean," I grumbled. "She likes to screw with me."

"Well, rest assured, Ross," Elle said, clapping my shoulder. "You're not the only one she won't listen too, so don't take it too personally."

I looked at Elle.

"She won't talk about her Ability with me either," Elle explained.

"Oh yeah, and there's that too," I muttered, and my discomfort nestled deeper.

Elle waved her words away. "Oh, don't worry. Kat's smart and more than capable, she'll do just fine in her new place. And," she said, holding up her index finger, "you're close enough to check on her whenever you want." Elle winked at me, and I glowered. I wasn't sure I liked the amusement in Elle's voice, but she was right. I was closer to Kat now, and there was a neighborhood of people around if she ever needed anything.

As Elle and I slowed at the pasture fence, I watched Kat and Thea together. Kat smiled as Thea picked at Puck's brown mane with a comb, struggling to reach high enough. But Thea wasn't so little anymore, and she only had to stretch onto her tiptoes. Her braided pigtails were gone, her long brown hair in a ponytail on top of her head instead, and for the first time in a while, I realized, she had all of her front teeth.

Now more than ever, I could feel how much things had changed, I just wasn't around as much anymore to notice—Thea wasn't a little girl anymore, Kat was moving out and potentially *dating*, and something was going on with Sophie.

I stopped just short of the pasture. "Are Alex and Sophie doing all right? Alex seemed . . . concerned about her and—"

"Oh," Elle flashed me a reassuring half-smile, and folded her arms over her chest in the cool breeze. "She's okay, just tired and, well, they've been going through a lot lately with the new house and her working at the school now. He's just being attentive."

It wasn't my place to pry, so I didn't, but it made me feel better that, whatever was going on, at least Elle knew about it. "You'll let me know if you need anything?"

A full smile parted Elle's lips and she snaked her arm through mine. "Yes, thank you." She leaned her head on my shoulder, and we looked at Kat and the girls as Thea and Aria each took one of Puck's reins and led him out of the pasture. He clomped happily closer, excitement in his eyes, but Kat hung back watching them, and her content expression wavered.

"Uh-oh," I muttered. I knew Kat's annoyed expression like the back of my hand, and as it mixed with a look of concern, I knew something was wrong.

"Hold up," Kat said, and with an indignant sigh, she walked over. Her heavy bootsteps crunching in the dirt punctuated the night air. "I can't ride him home tonight." She reached down and lifted Puck's hoof into her hand, bracing it on her knee. "He's lame. Looks like he stepped on something." She dropped his hoof with another sigh. "I need Jonathan to come out and take a look, make sure it's just a flesh wound and nothing more. The last thing I want is it getting infected."

"Does that mean Puck can stay longer?" Thea asked happily.

"Ha." Kat's eyebrow quirked slightly. "Luckily for you," she muttered, "yes. That's exactly what that means." She glanced at Elle. "If you don't mind."

"Of course not. Though, it does mean you'll need a ride

home." With too much delight, Elle looked at me. "Ross, you don't mind, do you? Since you live so close to each other now, I mean."

Kat looked between us, her face twisting with confusion. "Oh, so Ross needs convincing to do me a favor now?"

"No," I said as Elle chuckled. "Don't mind her." I met Kat's gaze and leaned closer. "I blame you for this."

Her lips parted in exasperation. "Me? For what?"

"For getting Elle tipsy. Now she's just being obnoxious."

Elle's laugh deepened. "I can't help it, I like messing with you when you're fussy."

Kat grinned. "It's fun, right?"

Glaring at both of them, I nodded to the truck. "Unsaddle your horse, Kat, and let's go," I told her, my voice gruff again. It tended to happen when I was around Kat, but Elle was full of piss and vinegar tonight too. I wasn't sure what she was insinuating or trying to do, exactly, but whatever Kat and I were, it was professional. We were partners, and perhaps our relationship loosely bordered on friendship, but nothing more. At least, that's the way I'd always thought about us. Between Kat and me, we had enough baggage to sink a ship.

FOUR
KAT

Ross and I drove in companionable silence as we turned off the bridge into Riverdale. The streetlights were on, thanks to the hydro plant, but the roads were quiet. The spring days were still short, and once the sun went down, there was little reason for anyone to be outside.

Ross passed the gym and apartment buildings and headed into the neighborhood all of us lived in. The houses and yards gave people a sense of normality, and vehicles and ATVs belonging to those who wanted them were parked in the driveways. Biodiesel had become easy enough to produce with the influx of community members, though not everyone wanted or needed means of transportation. Other than scavenging, there was no real reason to leave Riverdale.

I could take one of the patrol vehicles when I needed to, which I did from time to time, but I liked the quiet way of the world, and I preferred riding Puck or walking where I needed to go, if it was close. Living here was so different from the hustle and bustle of being on an Army base. Things were still fairly regimented, but it was slower and peaceful most of the time, and it was a nice change of pace.

My acre of land was like a buffer from the growing town. I didn't want someone like Meghann waving me down every chance she got, like Ross had to deal with, or people stopping to talk to me when I pulled into my driveway after a grueling day of work. I didn't want to worry about someone poking their head over the fence to say hello, or coming over to borrow a cup of sugar. I liked simplicity and peace and quiet, everything the world hadn't been before.

"Do you think Puck's pretty bad off?" Ross asked, turning down our street.

"No," I said with relief as I watched the houses pass by through the passenger window. "I don't think so. I doubt Jonathan will want me to ride him until his hoof is healed, though, just to be certain it doesn't get worse."

"Maybe Thea is trying to sabotage you." Ross didn't smile, but I could hear the jest in his voice. He had a dry humor I liked, even if I'd never tell him that.

"I wouldn't put it past her. I'd feel bad for taking him, except, knowing Jackson, Thea will get a horse by the end of the year if she wants one bad enough."

"It's not as easy as that, though—finding a trained horse, I mean. Especially one for a little girl to handle. Is it?"

"Thea's not so little anymore," I told him with a wry smile. "But you're right. For anyone else, it would be difficult to find one, but I know a guy." It was the same guy JJ and I had gotten our horses from in Hartley Bay. He was taking in horses that had been trained for trail riding and ranch work before the outbreak and had gotten a bit wild since. He used his animal telepathy to tame them again. "Some horses miss having human companions," I told him. "I can find her a good one when they're ready."

"Too bad Del's got Beauty now, that would've been a nice horse for Thea. I think JJ would've wanted her to have Beauty too."

The way Ross said JJ's name, like she was still a sore

subject, reminded me that even if Ross was overbearing a lot of the time, he was a big softy beneath the surface. What he'd done for JJ was proof of his compassionate heart, and even if I hated him for it the moment I found out she was dead, it hadn't taken me long to realize how selfless he'd been, taking her pain and suffering away to bear himself, so JJ didn't have to. His Ability was one I could hardly fathom.

"Yeah, it's too bad," I finally answered. "But this way, Thea will have something of her own. Not something leftover or handed down, like whichever wolf Beau isn't playing with, or a pet she has to share with the farm, like Big Red. And let's be honest. Aria is her friend, but she's more like Beau, she prefers animal companionship to people. I think Thea desperately wants that—a friend of her very own."

Thea was an easy kid to love, with a bubbly personality that outshined her grumpy brother even on her worst days, but I got the impression there was a lot more to Thea than the happy-go-lucky girl everyone saw. She didn't want to make waves or upset anyone; she was what people wanted her to be. I saw it in the way she clung to things—people, specifically. She never wanted to be left behind; always afraid she'd miss something. She hated to make people sad or upset, and she never complained, even when Beau picked on her or made her the butt of his jokes. I imagined Thea's need to be accepted was a lot like my need for simplicity. There was a comfort in it, a sense of security. While for me it was more like a chance to finally be my own person at the ripe age of thirty-two, for Thea, it was a reminder that she wasn't alone.

"She deserves something of her own," I mused. I saw an old soul in those amber eyes of hers, and I hoped that all she'd been through the past five years wasn't catching up with her. "I'll see if I can nudge Elle and Jackson to let her have one. They'll have an extra paddock once Puck is gone, anyway."

I could feel Ross's gaze on the side of my face.

"What?" I asked, refusing to look at him. I didn't know which expression I would find: the one he sometimes had when he looked surprised to discover I was human and cared about something, or the perturbed one because I'd said something too real or offensive.

"I've seen the way you are with Thea," he finally said.

"And how's that, exactly?" I stared out the windshield, at the empty street as we cruised down the road. The moon was out and bright in the sky, casting the interior of the truck in a wash of pale light.

"I don't know, she just looks up to you, I guess."

"Ha. I doubt that."

"I don't."

My gaze drifted to him. When Ross glanced at me, his deep blue eyes shimmered in the moonlight, and his red and brown stubble shadowed his features. "You don't give yourself enough credit, Kat," he said. "You—" Ross squinted out the windshield.

Strangely thwarted that he didn't continue, I glanced in the same direction and groaned inwardly. A familiar redhead flagged Ross down to pull over. "Here we go," I muttered.

Ross flashed me his trademark glare as he slowed the truck to a stop by the curb, and he rolled down his window. "Evening, Meghann."

"Well, here you are." Meghann's eyes shifted from Ross to me, skimming my face quickly, like she hadn't seen me a thousand times before, then she looked at Ross with a pretty smile parting her lips. "I didn't see you pass during your patrol, so I wasn't sure if something was the matter."

"No, not at all. Just changed things up a bit tonight to tend to some family stuff."

"Oh, well, that's a relief. Christine was telling me about the gangs in Edmonton and down south."

Fucking Christine. "So much for confidential," I grumbled, just loud enough for Ross to hear. Christine was methodical and smart on her feet, but she couldn't keep her mouth closed to save her life, a quality that was grounds for removal from the city council, if it were up to me anyway.

"Well, don't worry about any of that. We've got plans in place." Ross held the steering wheel with one hand and draped his left arm on the window frame. He was the picture of cool, calm ease and indifference, save for one thing—the way he rubbed the pad of his middle finger and thumb together, methodically, was a telltale sign he was anxious. It was one of a few nervous twitches he had that I'd picked up on over the years, which meant he probably liked Meghann, since she made him feel so uncomfortable. "I promise, you'll be plenty safe."

"Oh, good." Meghann patted her open palm on her chest, and I couldn't help but notice her scoop neck was a bit lower than usual. *Good grief.* I'd never realized just how annoying Meghann was until lately.

"You know," she continued. "I like to think the self-defense classes that Jamal's been teaching on Mondays and Thursdays are helping, but living alone is still new and a little frightening sometimes. I get so anxious being out here." Says the woman who could easily live in the apartment complex up the road, sharing a wall with her neighbors, if she was truly *that* concerned.

"I can understand that," Ross drawled. "But like I said, there's no immediate danger, and tomorrow we start moving forward with safety preparations." I liked that Ross pointed to me, including me in the *we*, like he hadn't forgotten I was sitting there. It was good that he thought of us as a team, because I did.

I also appreciated the way Meghann's brown eyes narrowed on me, as though she didn't like the reminder of my existence. I smiled at her politely. Even if Ross annoyed the shit out of me sometimes, he deserved better than sissy la-la Meghann Wyss. Ross was a good, hardworking man who turned this place into what it was with his devotion to this town and the people in it.

Meghann was just a bored gossip queen who liked to cook, and I didn't even know what else.

"Well," he started to say, then Christine and her pit bull, Samsonite, came into view down the street.

"Shit," Ross and I muttered in unison, and he looked at me. I hid my smile, and we waited impatiently for Christine to approach with an added spunk in her step when she noticed us parked on the curb.

I'd had enough of her in the past week to last me a lifetime, but I forced a half-pleasant smile. "Christine," I muttered in greeting as she stepped up beside Meghann. Her dog sniffed Meghann's butt, making Meghann wriggle in place a little, embarrassed, and I chuckled to myself.

"Ross. Kat." She nodded at us both, and she pushed her coke bottle glasses further up the bridge of her nose. "I was just talking about the gangs with Jamal. I've convinced him to add an additional self-defense class on Fridays." A wisp of her salt and pepper hair whipped across her face in the breeze, and she brushed it out of her face.

I rubbed my temple, knowing she was going to cause panic if she wasn't careful, and Ross and I would have to clean up her mess.

"I was thinking," she continued. "What if—"

"I appreciate your forethought, Christine," Ross said, interrupting her, and I could hear his patience thinning dangerously. "And I think the extra class is a good idea, *after* we meet with the council tomorrow afternoon. Okay? You've been back less than six hours. Why don't you go home and get some rest," he urged. "This can all wait until tomorrow. There's no need to get everyone worked up quite yet."

She smiled and huffed out a breath, as if the thought hadn't even occurred to her. "Well, I guess you're right." She sighed and nodded to Meghann, then to Ross and me. "I'll see you tomorrow then, Ross."

"Until tomorrow." He nodded at her as she waved and headed back in the direction she came.

"I'm just glad—" Meghann started, and Ross cut her off by looking up at the moon.

"I guess it's getting pretty late," he said with a charming grin. I hated that he flashed one at her, even if I didn't believe it was real. "I better get Kat home." Ross nodded up the road.

Once again, Meghann's eyes cut to me, then she forced a brittle smile between her lips. "Okay," she simpered. "Well, goodnight, Ross. I'll see you tomorrow."

With a dip of his chin, he put the truck into first gear.

"Wow," I muttered as we pulled away. I didn't wait for him to roll his window up, unconcerned whether or not Meghann could hear. "Obvious much?"

He glowered at me. "What?"

"Nothing." I bristled, suddenly anxious to be home.

"Well," he said, and proceeded to flash me a jovial smile, which didn't happen very often. His mustache lifted and gave way to a big, white grin.

"Well, what?" I glanced from him to the road, then back at him again. "Why are you smiling like that? You're being creepy."

Ross chuckled and pointed behind him in Meghann's direction. "You said no one would care or notice if I changed my patrol route and time." His eyebrows lifted. "You were wrong. I'm pretty sure you owe me a beer or something."

I rolled my eyes. "Meghann doesn't count."

"What? Why not? Of course she counts."

"No, she doesn't, because it's *Meghann*. She'd notice if you had a whisker out of place."

Somehow, that made Ross's grin widen. He angled himself to look at me more fully and glanced from the road to me. "Kat, is it just me, or do you sound a little bit jealous?"

"Oh, God. No. Don't start."

He chuckled, clearly pleased with himself. "Or, maybe you have a secret crush on someone," he said.

My eyes shot to his, and my heart thudded. "What?"

"Meghann," he prompted. His eyebrows rose suggestively.

I barked out a laugh. "No. Not in the slightest. Why the hell would you—" My laughter died away, and suddenly, I was acutely aware of the fact that Ross, and everyone else for that matter, *would* assume I liked Meghann, and I felt the nagging need to clarify. I cleared my throat. "I was with JJ, but that doesn't mean I don't like men." I could feel my cheeks burning crimson as I realized I was having this conversation with *Ross*. And as much as I didn't want to, I forced myself to look at him, my mind spinning in his silence.

He had a contemplative look on his face, and finally, he said, "Taylor, then?"

He asked it so seriously that I choked out another laugh. "What? No." I shook my head. "He's my friend, but I could knock him over with the flick of my finger. Besides, I think I intimidate him a little," I admitted.

But Ross only half-smiled, like he was too deep in thought. I wasn't sure what was going through his mind as he stared at me, but I couldn't handle the discomfort another minute. "Look, this is getting weird, and it doesn't matter anyway." I reached for the door handle. "I'm not trying to be with anyone, man or woman—"

Ross killed the truck engine as I opened the passenger door.

I frowned. "What are you doing?"

"I'm going in to make sure it's safe," he said, but I shook my head.

All embarrassment dissipated, replaced with annoyance. "Ross, it's fine. You've got enough to worry about. Besides, I have neighbors."

"Yeah, an acre away."

My gaze locked with his. "I'm serious. Would you pull this

crap if it were Bert or Phil living out here? I don't need you to see if it's safe for me. It is. And if it isn't,"—I patted the pistol in the holster at my hip—"I can take care of it. I'm perfectly capable."

"Yeah, but Kat—"

"Ross," I bit out.

His jaw clenched, illuminated by the interior light, but he didn't argue anymore as I slid out of his truck.

"Why won't you at least practice your Ability with Elle like she asked you to?" he grumbled in annoyance, and my gaze shot to his. "It might actually save you someday."

"Ross—"

"Kat."

"It's not your business," I told him. Rolling my eyes, I slammed the door. "Goodnight, Ross," I drawled, and headed up the path to my house. Ross and Elle didn't understand, and they needed to learn to leave things well enough alone.

FIVE
KAT

Jogging over to Ross's was part of the morning routine—wake up; drink a cup of tea, since it was more readily available than coffee; shrug into my workout clothes; and head to Ross's for an early morning workout session with the guys. So, that's what I did, only when I knocked on his front door, my chest heaving a little from my sprint over, Ross opened it in his sweatpants and nothing else save for the dog tag hanging around his neck.

His mug froze halfway to his lips. "Kat." He said my name with surprise, and I had to pry my gaze from the half-naked Ross in front of me. He worked out, I knew that much, but it was different seeing the sculpted muscles under his clothes, rather than just knowing they were there. It was harder to look at him as a work partner or a friend when he was standing there shirtless.

Gathering myself before things could get weird, I braced my hands on my hips and pushed into his house, forcing myself to ignore the awkwardness of my showing up, uninvited, apparently.

"Come in, why don't you," he muttered, and closed the door behind me.

I spun around, licking my lips as I made a point of looking only at his face. "You look like hell, boss. Didn't you get any sleep last night?"

He glared at me and took a sip from his mug. "Not exactly." He groaned and rubbed his hand over his head. "The bear was on the roam last night. He scared the shit out of me. I thought someone was breaking in."

"Uh-oh."

He waved my worry away. "He was playing with the damn garbage can on the side of the house."

I couldn't help but snicker.

"You laugh, but it's only a matter of time before he terrorizes you in the night," he warned.

"And you worry about *me* out there all by my lonesome. It sounds like you need a guard dog, Ross." I smirked.

"Yeah, or bear repellent."

As we stood in his living room with our hands on our hips, wrapped in awkward silence, my eyes darted to his naked chest again. "Well," I forced out with a shrug. "We're still working out, right? I mean, just because the rest of the guys are gone doesn't change anything."

"Uh, yeah. Sure."

I forced myself to look away and I turned for the backyard. I didn't like that I was suddenly aware of the broadness of his shoulders and the sporadic, deep red furls of hair on his pecs. "Throw some clothes on, would you? I'll warm up with the bag."

"Yeah, sure," he repeated. "It's not like it's my house or anything." Ross grumbled as his footsteps faded down the hall-way. Glad that was out of the way, I opened the back door and jogged down the steps to the screened-in porch, beelining for the punching bag.

Opening the trunk of workout equipment, I pulled out the gloves and shoved my hands inside. If I wasn't fully awake before, I was now.

Taking a deep breath, I let the crisp, early morning air fill my lungs and glanced around the porch. It was a fifteen by twenty-foot concrete slab, covered from the elements, but still cold as hell during the winter. Luckily, it was enclosed; probably someone's sunroom in another life. Now, it was *the pit*, our training room—usually filled with sweaty guys and me—complete with a punching bag, elliptical and rowing machines, a weight bench, and a jump rope area in the corner. It was the only unpacked, put together part of Ross's entire house, aside from his kitchen. At least, I think he had dishes and food in there. The only items I knew he had for certain were a water pitcher and a collection of coffee mugs that he rotated through.

Wiping away the loose hairs clinging to my face with the back of my arm, I widened my stance and began to punch. I was right-hand dominant, so it was all right jabs at first, then I forced myself to change to the left; careful not to let my elbow flare, and to keep the proper form Ross had practically beaten into me.

But even as I tried to focus, I wondered if I shouldn't have come. Phil, Jackson, Ross, and I worked out five days a week, that didn't change just because two of us were gone, did it? I tried not to feel like an idiot for assuming otherwise, even if Ross had.

The good thing was that I knew Ross had a weak jaw, and I could knock him a good one if he decided to give me any shit about it. I enjoyed the thought a little too much and continued punching.

Before I'd joined the police team we'd compiled, I could spar well enough to get a few good punches in; but thanks to the guys, I could do a lot more than that now. Specifically, thanks to Ross, I was twice as strong as I'd been before. I felt it in my arms and chest, in my shoulders, and even my forearms. While working out in the military had been a requirement, it was something I actually enjoyed doing with the guys.

By the time my arms were tinged with fatigue, Ross trotted

down the steps and into the workout area. He didn't spare me a glance as he pulled the covers off the weight machine and readied it for our session.

He wore the same thing he did every morning, rain or shine —loose shorts, tennis shoes, and a worn, oversized t-shirt. That was why seeing him shirtless had thrown me off, I realized. It made me feel a little bit better, like I wasn't a gaping ninny, but simply surprised. That was all. Any human with an appreciation for the fit male form would have noticed. Even if something else stirred inside me too.

"Here," I said, pulling the gloves off. We each had our own way of warming up. Mine was running, and loosening my muscles with the punching bag. Ross's was jump rope for cardio, and the bag. We both liked lifting weights after.

"Nice run this morning?" he asked, slipping his hands into the gloves. They didn't go on as easily, since his hands were bigger and less slender than mine, but I tried not to notice. I didn't know what the hell was wrong with me.

"Yeah, I guess." I changed the height of the seat on the leg machine and sat down, bending over to adjust the weight setting. "I like that the sun is rising earlier again."

"It won't be long before summer's here and everything kicks into hyperdrive."

"Yep." I lifted the first set, feeling my muscles, loose from the run, pull and burn a little with the weight. It was a satisfying feeling, one that always juiced me up in the morning, readying me for the day.

"I didn't think you'd come this morning," he huffed between jabs. The punching bag creaked with each strike. "I would've been more . . . prepared."

I upped the weight on the leg machine a little more, pushing myself a bit harder than usual to burn off the extra edge I was feeling. "I didn't mean to just barge in."

"Didn't you?" He glanced at me with a smirk, and reached for the punching bag, to hold it steady.

"Believe it or not, Ross—you're not the first thing on my mind when I wake up in the morning."

"Hmm."

I rolled my eyes and looked away.

Ross continued his warm-up of left and right jabs, a few hooks and bobs up and down; all in perfect form, of course. He didn't do anything half-assed. When I was finished, I rotated to the bench press so he could use the leg machine when he was ready.

"It's kind of nice not to have to listen to Jackson giving me shit about not moving all the way into my house yet," he said, steadying the bag again. He tugged the gloves off, dropped them back into the equipment trunk, and grabbed a hand towel draped over the jump rope hook.

"I don't know why he'd give you shit. You've only lived here a year. It's not like you've had time to move in or anything," I deadpanned and leaned back on the weight bench.

"Don't start with me," he grumbled.

"Oh, I'm not judging at all. In fact, *your* house in chaos makes me feel better about mine." I flashed him a goading smile, and reached above my head for the rubber grip on the barbell.

"Hey," he said nervously, and hurried over. The scent of deodorant and a hint of sweat settled around him as he towered above me. "You plan on having a spotter, or are you a complete rebel today?"

I blinked up at him. His chest still heaved a little from boxing, and his goatee, usually trimmed close to his jaw, was longer than usual, catching the sunlight peeking through the morning gloom.

His scolding blue gaze lingered on me a moment before flicking to my chest. His features narrowed to an almost-glare as he looked at me. "Well?"

My heart hammered a few more heartbeats as whatever was stirring inside me flared back to life like a struck match. I exhaled and tightened my grip on the bar, lifting it above my head. I concentrated on the strain of my biceps and the pull in my chest as I lowered it back down. Not on Ross or the unsettled look in his eyes. Not on my confusion or the uncertainty coiled in my abdomen. Instead, I exhaled it all again with the next lift, staring past Ross and at the ceiling, wondering what the hell had gotten into me, and how exactly, I was going to ignore it.

SIX
ROSS

Standing in my office at the makeshift police department, in what we were calling Downtown Riverdale, I stared at the overlapping maps of Whitehorse on my desk. I eyed an old, blown-up aerial view of the Riverdale neighborhood next. But the minutes I'd spent standing there, I wasn't thinking about the barricades or the gangs I *needed* to worry about, I was thinking about Kat.

We'd worked out together a hundred times over the past couple of years, and it had never felt so painfully uncomfortable between us as it did by the time she'd left this morning. I blamed it on Elle for putting ridiculous curiosities into my head—curiosities about Kat dating and why the idea of it bothered me so much; curiosities about Kat as a woman, not just my partner; and curiosities about her and me. Were Kat and I friends? It seemed a stupid question, and the answer was yes, but she wasn't the kind of friend I was used to having.

I leaned over and braced my palms on my desk. What the fuck was wrong with me? I'd never denied that Kat was attractive, and I had a lot of respect for her; she and I were a lot of things, but nothing romantic. She would never look at me like that, and yet, I hadn't stopped thinking about her since she'd left my house.

The front door creaked down the hall, and I straightened. "Sorry I'm late!" Kat called, and I heard the door swing shut. "I had to talk to Jonathan about Puck real quick." I could hear her rustling by her desk as I rubbed my temple. I would blame the bear and my lack of sleep for the distraction. "Hello?" she called.

"In here." I cleared my throat and stared at the doorway until she stepped into it.

"I brought coffee." She barely looked at me as she came into my office. Her eyes surveyed the maps on my desk, and she handed me a travel mug.

"Thanks," I muttered.

Kat took a sip from hers, and I noticed her wavy blonde hair was no longer in the ponytail she'd worked out in, but in that damn bun again, and her uniform was the same as it always was —a white long sleeve shirt that stretched over her chest just so, with tactical pants, boots, and her gun in the holster at her hip. Unlike most days, though, she was smiling more than usual, and her grin widened as I lifted the travel mug she brought me to my mouth.

I raised a skeptical eyebrow as I inhaled the scent of coffee. "It doesn't smell poisoned, but you're smiling like it is."

Kat rolled her eyes and took a sip of her own. "It's only arsenic."

I chuckled and took a pull of dark, freshly brewed roast. Kat wasn't one for friendly gestures, whether it be a hug or a simple early morning coffee pit stop at Taylor's shop. "You didn't make this, so let me guess . . . Rolland saw you walking into work?"

She touched her index finger to the tip of her nose. "Bingo. He *also* heard about the gangs from Christine, or maybe it was from Meghann," she said with a bit more of a bite. "Either way, he knows we have a lot of work to do, so he wanted to make sure we have sustenance."

"Damn that woman's mouth," I muttered.

"Tell me about it. And," Kat added, "I think he thought that if he plied me with coffee, I'd give him details. Only the joke's on him because my boss isn't very forthcoming with plans, so I had nothing to divulge."

"That's because I didn't have one until now," I told her.

Kat widened her stance and crossed her arms over her chest as she peered down at the unfurled maps again. "Okay then, what's the plan?"

"Well, it depends. Where do we want to start—the main entrance or the connecting bridge by your place, between the hydro plant and the fish ladder? The main entrance is more obvious, but the small bridge is closer to the neighborhoods—"

"Only if they're coming from the south, *and* if you know it's there," Kat pointed out. "It's not on any maps, and I don't see a band of reprobates taking a tour of the hydro plant anytime soon. The bridge into Riverdale, however, is more obvious. And if someone can sense body heat or Abilities, they'll know we're congregating here." She pointed to Lowes Boulevard. "I say we start the barricades here, at the main entrance, since it will be a larger project too."

I stared at her. It made sense, but it bothered me that she was closer to the other entry point.

Without glancing up from the map, she said, "You're looking at me funny again, I can feel it."

I forced my glare away. "It's nothing." I walked over to my desk and grabbed a notepad and pen. "Why don't you cross-reference the census to see which Abilities would be the most useful in the construction of the larger barricade? We'll vet a list, then make rounds to talk to people this afternoon and get them on board to help roll this project out as soon as possible."

Kat nodded. "Sure thing, boss," she said, knowing I hated it when she called me that. "What are you going to do?"

"I need to make a list of materials we'll need and figure out if we have them here, or if we have to make a trip."

"Got it. I'm on it." Kat took a sip from her coffee and headed toward her desk in the front. She was the lead of our makeshift command center of sorts, in an old office building at the edge of the neighborhood. It was a more centrally located and smaller, satellite version of what we had at the prison. City council was held in the conference room down the hall, and while Jackson and I shared an office, Kat and Phil shared the front.

There wasn't a single word on my list of supplies when I heard the crash of the front door open. "Ross!" Beau's voice rang out, and I jumped out of my chair and ran into the hall. Beau glanced around with wide, shimmering blue eyes.

"What is it?" Kat said, jumping up from her desk.

"Sophie said to hurry, something's wrong with Mrs. Filmore." She was the other, older teacher who had been ailing since she came to our settlement over a year ago.

"Shit." Absently checking for my gun, I ran from the building, into the gray morning. For the hundredth time, I was grateful our hamlet was still small enough that everything was so close.

Sprinting across the street, I leaped over the curb and rushed into the elementary school building we were using to teach all grades. Kat and Beau were somewhere behind me as I followed the anxious cries and pleas of the students in the classroom down the hall.

"Out of the way," I told them as I rushed inside. I moved Thea out of the way to find Mrs. Filmore lying on the ground, her eyes barely blinking as she looked dazedly around the classroom. It was her lungs. No doubt they were finally giving up on her; and as I grabbed for her discarded oxygen, she meekly lifted her hand, pushing mine away. Her head lulled to the right and the left in defiance as her eyes rolled back into her head.

"What's happening?" Thea whimpered.

"Is she dying?" another girl squeaked. The kids were crying and demanding reassurance as Sophie tried to usher them out of the room.

The moment Kat ran in with the first aid kit in her hand, I nodded for her to help Sophie with the kids. "And shut the door," I told her, wanting to be locked inside with the dying old woman, alone.

Kat hesitated. "But, Ross—"

"Do it, Kat," I commanded, and then I refocused on Mrs. Filmore as she took a shaky, shallow breath. "Here you go," I whispered, and placed a balled-up jacket beneath her head. It was better than the linoleum flooring.

I could feel it on her, the heavy cloud of death against her chest and filling her mind. Mrs. Filmore didn't have long. I stood and pulled the shawl off the back of her desk chair, then crouched back down and draped it over her to help stave off some of the chill.

"It will be okay, Mrs. Filmore," I breathed, staring into her glassy, gray eyes. "It will be okay." I squeezed her hand, hating what I knew would come the moment I let it in, but I knew what Mrs. Filmore had been through—all that she'd lost, and how she'd been suffering to survive ever since the outbreak. She'd reached her end, and I was going to make it as painless as I could for her.

Holding her hand against my chest, I nodded. "Breathe with me," I said softly, feeling the coolness of her clammy hands seep into mine. "That's it . . . You'll feel better soon."

Letting Mrs. Filmore's soul into mine triggered a domino strand of images from the lives I'd felt before—what was left of Kelsey's shattered soul as it left this world; JJ's pain, and her heart, riddled with unrest—and my eyes blurred with a broken dam of emotions. Regret. Relief. Longing. Anguish. Anger.

I felt the wash of desperate sadness and fear as Mrs. Filmore learned her husband wasn't coming back from the Korean War decades ago, and she'd be a single mother of four. I felt the misery and sickening sense of loss as her ailing granddaughter, who she'd raised, lay in a lifeless heap in her arms after losing a battle with cancer. I felt her relief in knowing she would soon see her again, and I allowed Mrs. Filmore to hold on to that peace as what little life was left in her leached from her body, through me, and into nothing. I took away the cold, and I took away the darkness, until all she could feel was weightless relief.

The instant Mrs. Filmore was gone, the heaviness inside of me lightened, though the toll had been taken. My mind and heart were a roiling storm, my limbs heavy with exhaustion. I felt like a punching bag, battered by assaulting memories. My stomach churned and my body hummed with the influx of energy, and I leaned against the desk.

"Ross . . ." Kat's voice was small beside me and riddled with apprehension.

Opening my eyes, I watched as she covered Mrs. Filmore's ashen face with the shawl.

Knowing I couldn't sit in the middle of class a crumpled heap, I dropped Mrs. Filmore's hand and struggled to climb to my feet.

"Here," Kat said, straining under my weight as she used her body to support me. I hated that she even had to help me, that I felt weak, and yet, Kat was a welcome warmth against the iciness of my skin.

It had been three years since I'd done something like that. Three years since JJ's death, and seeing the look of horror and hatred burning in Kat's eyes. I dreaded to look at her again for fear of what I'd see in them now. But I did, and it wasn't hatred this time, but sympathy as she watched my body shake.

"You didn't have to do that," she said as I braced myself against the edge of the desk.

"I wanted to," I told her. She rested her hand on my shoulder, though I wasn't sure it was *want* so much as what I felt compelled to do because I could.

"You give me shit about not practicing and being reckless with my Ability—"

"That's completely different."

"No, it's not. And you can't go around doing that for everyone. You have no idea what toll it really takes on you and—"

My eyes shot to hers. "It's my burden to bear," I told her, and with a sigh, I shook my head. "I just—need a minute, okay?" Every nerve felt like it was buzzing with emotion overload, and my body hummed as it all came too close to the surface. I felt light-headed and sat on the desk. "Don't let the kids in here yet," I told her. The last thing I wanted was a rush of tears and shrieks. "We need to get Mrs. Filmore out of here—"

"I'll deal with it," she said, more coldly than before. "Just . . . sit down before you fall over and I have to explain to them why the chief police officer keeled over too." She pushed Mrs. Filmore's chair over to me.

As I lowered myself into it, I heard Kat sigh. "Ross," she whispered, and I hated how frail I felt under the weight of her concern.

"Just give me a minute, okay, Kat?" I said, rubbing my temple.

She stared at me; I could feel her gaze burning a hole in the back of my head. "I'll tell Sophie to keep everyone in the hallway until you're ready for them to come in," she finally said, a little roughly. "And don't worry about Mrs. Filmore. I'll get Rolland, he can help me move her."

Squeezing my eyes shut, I nodded. Tears stung the backs of my eyes as the frenetic energy inside me fed off every nerve ending; all-consuming in a way I hadn't felt in so long, it was harder to push it away.

"Ross—"

"Go, Kat!" I snapped, over my shoulder.

"Fine. Sorry for caring," she muttered. Without another word, Kat stepped out into the hallway, shutting me inside with Mrs. Filmore and a head-splitting feeling of regret.

57

SEVEN
KAT

With a fortifying exhale, I sat down on the curb outside the school. My hands wouldn't stop shaking and my palms were sweating. I could've passed it off as adrenaline from the last thirty minutes, but that would've been a lie. It wasn't until I realized what Ross was going to do that I felt a cold veil of fear fall over me, and an unexpected foreboding thought followed: *What would it do to him?*

I'd met Ross when he was coming out of the darker part of his life, when he started finding purpose and really living his life again. Since then, I'd learned only a couple of things about him, but they were things that made him . . . Ross.

First, he shouldered more than any one man should, taking the blame for things that were out of his control and making everything and everyone his problem to bear. Whitehorse was the perfect example of that; it would be only half of what it was without him.

And he was selfless. He didn't realize it, and if I knew Ross as well as I thought I did, he probably felt he needed to do more and work harder than he already did, as if he was always atoning for a misdeed. Maybe it had to do with Kelsey, or the people whose lives he'd taken in the Army, which I knew next to nothing about, or maybe it was the people he hadn't helped after he learned what he could do. Either way, his selflessness was annoyingly gallant, but more than that, it had no bounds, and I saw the impact it had on him, even if he didn't. The drinking binges, when he was too overwhelmed to cope with simply breathing—the walls he built around himself, which was why we got along so well, or rather, why we could tolerate each other. Regardless, I couldn't shake the fear that Ross using his Ability would pull him further away from everyone again, further away from me, and the fact that it mattered so much that it left my stomach in knots, scared me the most.

"Hey," Sophie said softly behind me. She stopped at the curb and lowered to sit beside me. "You okay?" Her long hair fell over her shoulder as she leaned in.

"Yeah, sure. Just annoyed." I did a double take. "Shouldn't you be inside with your students?"

She shrugged. "They're fine. I filed them into Steve's classroom. They get to sit with the big kids for a while, so they're too excited to be anxious."

"Ah, clever." I studied her a moment. "And you? How are you holding up?"

"Fine, just a little unsettled, I think."

"Yeah, that's a word for it." I inhaled, long and deep, and peered out at the vacant downtown. We only had a couple hundred citizens, compared to the thousands that used to live here, and a small part of Riverdale was all we needed, with housing and a few businesses to make it feel adequate.

Taylor's shop, two buildings to the right, provided a little bit of everything to the townspeople—from bread and produce traded with Prince Rupert, to the local preserves and handmade clothing that some citizens excelled in making here.

The Outpost, where citizens requested trade goods from down south and offered up wares of their own for trading, was in the building beside it. And down the road was the hospital; only a small medical wing was used and run by Nathan, a dermatologist before the outbreak, and his willing apprentice, Sadie.

There were other small establishments, like the mechanic shop, which was well manned, given our low demand for vehicle services, though they helped with plows and larger equipment as well. A handful of other homes served as personal offices; like for Jonathan, the veterinarian; and for Kathy, the piano teacher, who welcomed anyone wanting to learn into her home for scheduled sessions. Everyone did what they could to contribute and keep busy, and when they had no specific desires or capabilities, they worked in the community garden or cleaned the empty houses, readying them for newcomers. Some citizens helped tutor kids in their studies since the school was full and the teachers were few, and others floated around to whatever projects needed help. The rest of our little Riverdale neighborhood fanned out to the left.

At least people were learning how to move on with their lives, and again, a lot of that was possible because of Ross.

I peered across the street at the police station. It was boxy and dreary and smelled like mildew half the time, but it was ours and it was routine, and I liked it.

"Ross is okay," Sophie said softly. "I mean, he'll be okay, eventually."

I forced myself to look at her. Even if I didn't say anything, Sophie was observant and smart, and I hated that she probably knew what I was thinking without me saying a single word. "It's the *eventually* part I don't like," I told her.

"He's already doing better than he used to after something like this."

"Or he's hiding it better," I countered. "He has a town to look after now, things are different." Ross wouldn't jeopardize the safety of the people here and go on a binger, even if that's exactly what he needed. He'd still shoulder everything he felt was his to bear and suffer the effects of it. It wasn't healthy.

Sophie's lips pursed, but she didn't deny it, which made me feel worse. She knew him better than any of us—she knew all of us better than the rest—and what she didn't say about Ross made the unease almost viscous.

"I liked Mrs. Filmore, so don't get me wrong when I say this," I started, "but we all knew she didn't have much longer. She was old, and everyone dies—what's he going to do, siphon the souls of every single person as they take their last breath? Is that his role now?"

When Sophie didn't acknowledge my question, I met her gaze. "Why does it bother you so much?" she finally asked. "If that's what he decides to do, I mean."

"Because what kind of life is that?" I practically screeched. "No one *wants* that. I mean, do you like seeing Ross half-dead and in anguish? I sure as hell don't." I thought about the look on his face when I'd found him standing by JJ's bedside, after helping her find peace with her last breath.

I folded my arms across my knees and shook my head. "Doesn't he get a second chance like everyone else has gotten, or is he doomed to be the Grim Reaper for the rest of his life? And he'll do it too, you know he will." I remembered how much I hated him at first, especially in that split-second of realizing JJ was gone, and that he was the one who'd taken her from me. I'd unleashed my pain and anger on him, and he'd taken it willingly.

"I hate what I did," I said aloud for the first time. "The day I came back and she was gone, Ross didn't deserve that. He doesn't deserve any of this. He's a good man, even if he annoys the shit out of me most of the time."

"You can't beat yourself up for what happened back then, Kat. No one blames you, especially not Ross."

"That's my point," I muttered.

"He knows what it's like to lose someone you care so much about."

"Still, it feels like shit," I grumbled, and flicked a pebble on the asphalt across the street.

"I knew you cared about him," Sophie said, her voice was a thoughtful whisper. "But I don't think I realized how much."

I frowned, disliking the burn in my cheeks as her meaning sank in, but I played it off. "Why, don't you? He's like a brother to you, or an uncle or something."

"Of course I do." Her lips twitched with a barely-there smile, and she shrugged. "But it's different for me."

Cocking my head, I waited for her to continue. When she didn't, I shifted to face her fully, feeling my defenses rise a little. "What's that mean, exactly?"

Her eyebrows rose. "You tell me."

I bit my lip, my mind foreign to me as I tried and failed to formulate the words. "I just—" I was beginning to realize I cared about Ross more than I probably should, but he and I were like oil and water. Not to mention, he was a stubborn asshole who grated on my nerves every chance he could. "Never mind. Maybe he doesn't want a second chance in life or a shred of happiness. What the hell do I know."

"There's the bitter Kat I know and love," she jested, and I snorted a laugh. "Is that why you want to take the serum so badly?"

My smile fell. "What do you mean?"

"Do you think that will help you put everything behind you, so you can have a real second chance at happiness?"

Clenching my jaw, I tried not to be angrier than I already was. "He told you about the serum too?"

With a weary smile, she shook her head. "Do you really have to ask that?"

I swallowed, feeling strangely relieved, and realized I was getting too worked up, and it was all for nothing in the end.

"No," I said, rolling my eyes. "I don't have to ask, and I'm pretty sure my demons will haunt me regardless of any serum I take, actually." I eyed her skeptically. "When are you going to be able to see into the future too? That would be more helpful than rummaging around in the past every time you touch someone."

Laughing, Sophie leaned back and held her face up to the sun as it peeked through the clouds. "It's funny," she mused, her eyes flitting shut. "We all still want things we can't have, even though we've all been given a new start, and we have all of this now." She gazed around at our little community; vastly different from the desolate ruin it had been after the outbreak.

"All of us?" I chuckled. "I don't want to hear about it, Sophie. You've got Alex, and soon you'll have a new home. You've got family, and a job you love here at the school . . . You have everything you could possibly want. The rest of us, yes— I'll admit I want more, but I've always wanted what I can't have, so . . ." I shrugged with a self-deprecating laugh, but Sophie didn't join in. She didn't have a quippy comeback or counter-argument as I'd expected, either. Instead, the easiness of her expression faltered and she sat up, brushing her palms off on her thighs.

I sobered, feeling that nagging sense of unease settle in again. "What?" I'd only been partially joking with her. I knew no one's life was ever perfect, but as far as I knew, Sophie and Alex were happy; they were settled and embracing their new lives with more gusto than the rest of us.

"I don't have everything I want," she said quietly. "And I'm not sure I ever will."

Instinctively, I knew what she was referring to, and that she hadn't said anything sooner made my heart ache for her. "You don't have to tell me, but—"

"It's fine," she said with a forced smile. She picked at her fingernail. "I don't mind, but only Elle and Alex know so far." She cleared her throat. "I was pregnant," she whispered. *Was.*

My heart plummeted, and the longing in her voice made my eyes burn with unshed tears. "I was scared at first," she continued, "petrified, actually. All I could hear were my mom's words playing over and over in my head about responsibility and how a kid would be a huge undertaking, especially in the world we're living in now. I even thought it was irresponsible for a moment." Sophie let out a breath and wiped the moisture from beneath one of her eyes. "Elle helped me come around to the idea, and, I dunno, I got excited about it—*we* got excited. It felt like Alex's and my story had finally come full circle, and it felt so right and meant to be, I was more ecstatic than I've ever been. Now," she shook her head. "Now it's just . . . hard."

"I'm sorry, Sophie." The words were inadequate, but I didn't know what else to say. Suddenly, her fear of the gangs made more sense. I assumed parenthood or the thought of it did that, made you look at the world through a different lens, one that made it seem more dangerous than it already was. "Have you thought about trying again?"

With a shrug, she ran her fingers through her hair and finally looked at me. "Yeah, and we sort of have, but it's scary, you know? Maybe it's not safe since we have no idea what's really going on in our bodies after all the changes. And if something went wrong during the pregnancy . . . I don't know what we'd do. Maybe it's just not meant to be, like we thought."

I hadn't thought of that. The Virus changed us, but what did that mean, exactly? I knew there were some people who had had children in the past few years, but there weren't many, and it was too soon to tell what the effects would be on a grand scale.

"So, you see?" she said, rallying with a small smile. "I want a family of my own, which I may never get. And you want to control your new life, since you've never had the chance to before, and you want Ross to be happy—something you can't control."

With a haughty laugh, I shook my head. "God, I hate that you know everything. You're like a walking life coach or some-thing." Sophie laughed, a real laugh this time, and I smiled too. "You should just offer therapy at this point, and have people pay you in books and whatever nerdy things you like."

"Ha! Definitely not."

We rose to our feet, brushing off our backsides as we prepared ourselves to face the music inside. I had never wanted to have a child; at least I'd never had the physical need to do so. I wasn't mother material anyway. The fun, foul-mouthed aunt maybe, but not a mother. "Are you going to be okay?" I asked, wishing there was something I could do for her.

"Yeah, I'll be fine. I've had some time to come to terms with it, and I know I'm lucky to have my life, even if what happened is disappointing."

We stood there in silence for a few moments. The wrens chirping from the spruces that grew sporadically down the street.

Maybe it was because I felt like I had friends—true friends—for the first time in my life, but I wanted them to be happy, almost protectively so. We all deserved it, even if I wasn't naive enough to wish it for myself.

"I *am* happy," Sophie said so quietly, I barely heard her. A small smile curved her lips. "You will be too."

"More predictions?" I asked.

She looked at me, her smile widening to a grin. "Not a predi-cation," she said. "A fact."

I shook my head. "From now on, I'm just going to assume you're omniscient," I told her.

Sophie chuckled softly again, and with a heavy breath, I nodded toward the station. "I have some work to do. Let Ross know if he asks, would you?" The last thing I was going to do was bother him again.

"Sure."

As I turned to head across the street, Sophie called my name.

I zipped around. "Yeah?"

"I know you're worried about Ross, but our Abilities are . . . difficult. You don't want to embrace yours, and I understand why, but it's different for Ross and me." She glanced around like she was searching for the right words. "For us, it's not about doing and thinking, it's about feeling—for him especially. Whatever toll it takes on him, it would be much worse if he did nothing at all. He'll never find the peace you think he deserves that way."

Even if Sophie's words made sense, my heart still ached for him. As she turned back for the school, I reminded myself that if I'd learned anything in the past few years, it was that I couldn't control other people. Ross and JJ were no different in this; there was nothing I could do about Ross and the decisions he made, just like I hadn't been able to control JJ's. I had to accept whatever Ross wanted to do with his life, no matter how much it pained me to watch, or the helplessness I felt in its wake.

EIGHT
ROSS

I pulled the truck into the small parking lot, glad to see the Tahoe was there. Even if I was still groggy from yesterday at the school, I couldn't stay cooped up in my house another minute. Exhaustion was something I was used to, and I ignored the heaviness of it in my muscles as I climbed out of the truck. The last thing I needed to do today was dwell a moment longer on the full life I felt through an old woman's memory, and compare it to the sad state of my own. A nice squabble with Kat would be a welcome distraction.

As I walked to the front of the building, I eyed the school across the street, noting that some of the teens were out in the gated yard, eating their lunch. I didn't think about the youth in Whitehorse all that much, other than there were a lot of them—more than there were adults. And I definitely didn't think about how life was for them now, after everything that had happened. What had they been through? How horrible had it been for some of them? I could assume and imagine a lot. Were they acclimating now? I had no idea, and as I thought about the miscreant kids trolling the woods, I wondered if these young survivors realized how lucky they were to have a place like this.

When I pulled the door open, Kat peered up from a mess of maps and folders opened on her desk, but she only spared me a quick glance before she looked back down at the binder in front of her. "Hey, boss." She flipped through the pages, scanning them with her index finger. However unproductive my morning had been, stewing in a mental haze at home, it looked like she'd been busy at least.

"Kat," I answered, and the cool afternoon air rushed in as the door shut behind me. "We should probably get that list finished up so we can—"

"I did, and I reached out to Jamal, Kev, and Smitty—they're all on board to help out with Barricade One. They said to name the day and place, and they'll be there."

"Oh." I shrugged my jacket off and hung it on the coat rack. "I'll go finish up the rest of the sketch then, see what supplies we still need—"

"I put something rough on your desk to look at," she said distractedly. "You'll probably want to redo it, but you can decide when you see it."

Kat didn't fuck around when it came to her job, but I was surprised, or maybe a little let down, that she'd done so much without me.

"Is there anything you *haven't* done?" I asked tersely. "Or are you taking the chief job now too?"

Kat glanced up at me again, and I felt my cheeks redden. "That was an asshole thing to say. Sorry."

Her eyes lingered on mine a few seconds longer, then she looked away.

I took a step closer to her desk. I didn't know what my problem was, only that she was the last person I wanted to piss off right now, especially after our interaction yesterday. "Thank you for getting all of that done for me."

"Sure." It was a curt, rushed response. She flashed me a forced, forgiving smile.

Rubbing my temple, I turned for the hall. "You know where to find me, if you need me."

"Sure thing." Kat rose from her seat, and when I heard the jingle of keys, I looked back. She pushed her long sleeves up to her elbows, the Tahoe keys in her hand.

"Where are you off to now?"

Kat closed the inventory binder on her desk and slid it into the row with the other binders and references she maintained. "I'm going to grab Jonathan and take him out to look at Puck. I left the list of materials I think we'll need on your desk with the sketch. We can finalize them tomorrow. Or whatever you think is best." She flashed me another forced smile. "Call me on the radio if you need me." She brushed past me and opened the front door.

"Wait, you're not coming back today?"

Kat looked back at me. "It depends."

"On what?"

"On whether or not Nathan and I get finished digging Mrs. Filmore's grave for tomorrow's service."

She said it so matter-of-factly, like helping Nathan at the hospital was a normal thing for her to do, I almost felt like I was being dense for a minute.

"If not, I'll see you tomorrow." Kat turned and disappeared out the door like she couldn't get away fast enough.

It didn't take a genius to grasp how upset she was with me. I'd clearly hurt her feelings by pushing her away yesterday, and I felt an unexpected rush of panic as I realized that she was now shutting me out, and there was no one but myself to blame.

NINE
KAT

As I stood in my living room, staring at the three unopened boxes stacked beside the fireplace, my hands ached from shoveling with Nathan all afternoon. Unlike my cabin at Elle's, it felt more like I was squatting here. I hadn't really taken the time to move in fully, but then, I didn't have much to begin with—a fact that hadn't bothered me until now. I was angry with Ross for reasons that made no sense, worried about his second chances when I hadn't done much to embrace my own. The last thing I wanted was for a year to go by and to still be living out of boxes, like he was.

I thought about what Sophie had said, about the serum giving me a reason to truly start fresh; she was right. If three boxes of crap, and my clothes haphazardly placed in the bedroom closet, were all I had to show for the past three years, it was pretty pathetic.

Maybe I hadn't had the time to unpack, or maybe I just lacked the motivation to settle in fully, but I had both now. I needed to keep my mind busy, so I wouldn't waste another minute worrying about everyone else. Between the funeral tomorrow, Puck, and the barricades; there were plenty of things to keep my mind preoccupied while I figured my own shit out and let Ross deal with his.

Now, it was finally time to unpack, and the tightness in my chest told me I needed to brace myself for it. Everything I had was mine—*my* things in *my* house. If I allowed myself to settle here, actually *settle* some place for the first time in my life, it might be the first step to truly starting over.

I peered around the small, two-bedroom cabin. It was furnished with a coffee table and two mismatched side tables; a mahogany leather couch with a folded flannel blanket on the back; a worn, overstuffed recliner beside the fire; and a kitchen table with three high-backed chairs that looked like something an old hunter had made himself, with gnarled wood and unfinished edges. A shriveled welcome bouquet of fireweed and wild dandelions sat in the center of the table, surrounded by fallen, withered flower petals. Marianne, a former dispatcher and our resident green thumb, was on the cleaning and welcome committee for new members. I'd have to thank her when I saw her next for getting the place straightened up for me. And the flowers were a sweet touch, even if I wasn't home enough to enjoy them.

This house was all I needed for now; a blank slate to start my own life, whatever that meant or looked like. I didn't want to be a burden on Elle and Jackson anymore, and if I was honest, being around Elle all the time made it difficult to move on. Not because she looked like JJ, but because everything had changed when JJ and I finally met up at Elle's place. JJ's health and our relationship had gone from not that great to even worse in a matter of days, and I needed to close that chapter of my life for good. It was over; JJ was gone. She'd chosen death over life, and there was nothing I could've done about it. At least, that's what I kept telling myself.

Pulling my knife from my pocket, I sliced open the box on the top of the stack and folded the flaps open, instantly smiling.

The drawing Thea had sketched a couple of years ago, of me on top of Puck, was creased a bit and lying right on the top.

Good, artwork. I needed a little something to liven the place up. Bending back the folded edges, I walked the drawing over to the refrigerator and used a Terminix magnet to hold the drawing in place. I made a mental note to scrounge up some new magnets one of these days, and walked back over to my things.

Everything inside of the box smelled like my old cabin at the farm—smoke from the wood-burning stove, and cinnamon from my lotion. Cracked hands, from the dry cold, weren't something I had ever acclimated to, even after all the years I'd been in Juneau and Anchorage. Fleetingly, I wondered if my life before the military and the General had been someplace warm.

I pulled out my sketchpad and skimmed through the pages of notes and names of people I'd heard about during the months I'd spent searching for a cure. Some of the writing was legible, some of it wasn't. There were water stains from the nights I'd stayed up, silently crying and pleading for a way to make it all better. All the while, I had been the answer I was looking for the whole time.

I'd heard rumors of Re-gens while I was stationed in Juneau, but that's all they'd ever been to me—horror stories that soldiers only whispered about when they'd had too much to drink and had loose tongues. I'd never met one, let alone did I know how they were created. Or that I'd inadvertently create one myself.

The day I brought JJ back to life had been accidental in every sense. She was dying—dead, even—and I was a despondent heap of nothing, willing her to come back with every fiber in me. I feared life without her, after the years we'd spent together; I feared who I might become, and I feared the unknown as the world crumbled around me. More than anything, I was terrified of myself and of the missing pieces I'd have to face alone.

After JJ had taken her final breath, on that stretcher in the back of an unmarked van outside the Whitely apartment complex, something both horrifying and miraculous happened. From some deep, despairing part of me, I wished her back to life. I hadn't realized what I was feeling at first—only my determination, and an electrical charge that hummed through my tendons and out my fingertips. It made my skin tingle, and my tongue burn like I was touching it to the tip of a charged battery.

And as the thick, stormy air pulsed in the evening sky, I could feel the electricity in the air, sparking around me until a flash, so bright it almost blinded me, struck down between us, pushing us apart.

Dazed in the beginning, I panicked, uncertain what had happened. It felt like Zeus himself had struck me from the sky. I still felt the muted itch of it inside me sometimes. When I saw my handprints burned into JJ's chest and realized her heart was beating, I froze, horrified. Like Frankenstein's monster, JJ was suddenly alive—unconscious, but alive.

And while it was the most miraculous day of my life, I knew the moment she woke—with gray, clouded eyes, uncertain who I was—that somehow, I'd done something terrible. JJ lived and breathed, but she was different, and with each memory she reclaimed and each use of her Ability, she weakened. How could I ever want that for someone again?

Pulling the framed photo of us from the box, I rose to my feet. It was still hard to reconcile how little she remembered of our relationship, or that she didn't fight to be with me. I understood it in a way, the utter exhaustion of living, but I still felt the sting of not being enough, even if I'd learned to move past it.

I placed the frame on the left side of the fireplace mantel, grateful all over again that Elle had given it to me. But there was another photo I wanted to find, one that, strangely, meant even more to me.

Going back to the box, I shuffled through a few books; one romance novel Elle insisted I read, *His Untamed Desire,* though I hadn't bothered to crack it open yet; and a couple of first aid and engineering books I referenced frequently, specifically when it came to working on projects with Bert.

Then, I saw it. The intricate metal, framing the photo of the entire crew the day we'd left for the first summit. My gaze skimmed over Elle and JJ standing at the end, a forced smile on JJ's face, but a smile identical to Elle's nonetheless. Bert wasn't looking at the camera, and Jackson looked like he might actually be chuckling, probably at something Woody had said, based on Woody's dopey grin. I glanced at Phil and Sophie, and a small-smiled Alex, before my eyes landed on buzzed-haired, blue-eyed Ross, squinting into the sun with a full smile beside Beau.

When I'd first met Ross, he was an overbearing and distrusting dark cloud, while all I'd wanted was for JJ to be happy. It wasn't until months later that I realized what kind of man Ross really was. Stronger than he needed to be, fiercely protective of his friends and family, and he carried the weight of the world on his shoulders. Ross was still a killjoy some of the time, but I was beginning to think I liked that about him, it was an austere shell of self-preservation, and I could relate to that.

I jumped at the clanking sound of my garbage can out back. "Damn it, Bear," I muttered. I never thought I'd have to scold a grizzly bear before. Rising to my feet, I set the picture frame in the center of the mantel and headed to the back door with my hand on my gun, just in case. Flicking on the porch light, I peered into the backyard, seeing only the deck, and my garbage knocked over and rolling in the breeze.

A storm was coming, I could feel it alive on my skin, and I had a feeling that Bear could sense it too. He'd only been out of torpor a few weeks, and after being confined for the cold months of winter, any animal, including me, would be restless.

I opened the sliding door. There was a rumble of thunder in the distance, and I gripped the hilt of my pistol as I made my way outside, peering around for a giant grizzly. "Aria better get you under control, or I swear—"

I stopped in my tracks, wondering if my eyes were playing tricks on me as I drew my pistol. The outline of a teenager flashed a few feet or so in front of me, then disappeared. Before I could process it, something hard and heavy hit my temple.

I fell to the ground as the world spun, and the back of my head throbbed. "Jesus . . ." I blinked as my vision began to blur, and just before my eyelids flitted shut, a young boy flickered into existence above me again. Then, another boy stepped into view, and together they peered down at me, smiling, before everything faded to black.

TEN

ROSS

"Come on, kid," I said, climbing out of my truck. "I'm going to grab something from my house, then we'll make the rounds." I was feeling better than I'd felt this afternoon, even if the muddled sensations and memories from yesterday still lingered a little. I'd had the urge to drink, but I knew that couldn't be my escape anymore, so I worked late instead. Coping was something I still needed to work on, and remind myself of the next time I decided to pull the trigger and let death in. Of course, I would do it again; I wasn't sure I could live with myself if I didn't, knowing I could've eased a good person's final moments. Even if I hated that I could.

Beau climbed out of the passenger side of the truck as Luna jumped out of the back, both of their manes blowing in the wind. When we got inside, I handed Beau a flannel to shrug into, and he blinked at me. "We're not walking, are we?"

"Yes, we are," I told him, and I beelined for the fridge, where I'd put a bottle of homebrew to chill after work.

Beau glanced around the living room and the furrow in his brow deepened. "This is your house? Why are there so many boxes?" The place was less homey than he was used to, I'd give him that. "I thought you moved here like, a year ago or something."

"Yeah, well," I said, setting the 22-ounce bottle of beer on the counter. I grabbed my jacket off the back of a chair at the kitchen table. "I guess I haven't gotten settled in yet." The truth was, anywhere to sleep was better than nowhere, but that didn't mean it was home.

Beau eyed the beer bottle. "Are you going to get drunk?"

"No, it's not for me, kid." It wasn't a ludicrous question, even if I thought the assumption formed a little too easily. "It's a peace offering for Kat. It's her favorite thing to drink on her days off."

"Why do you need a peace offering?"

I checked the Glock magazines on my belt holder and pulled on my jacket, ready to start patrol. "I need to get back on Kat's good side. I was sort of a jerk yesterday, and she's sort of avoiding me at the moment." I nodded toward the front door. "Come on, let's make the rounds quick tonight. It's going to rain."

The truth was, I needed the fresh air. I wasn't sure why Kat caring what I did with my Ability had affected me so much, but it did, and after working at only half capacity since yesterday, I needed to burn off some energy, and the brisk air was my only option at the moment. Plus, I had to figure out what, exactly, I was going to say.

Beau and Luna followed me out the door, and I locked it behind us. "If it's going to rain, wouldn't driving be better?" he asked as he hurried down the path toward the sidewalk to keep up with me. "And wouldn't we cover more ground if we were in the truck?"

"Yes, we would, and everyone would see and hear us coming a mile away, too. This way, we can be discrete. There's no point in patrolling if everyone can hear you coming. Besides, this part of Riverdale is small, we can manage it in under an hour."

"Well, if it rains, Elle's going to be pissed. She hates the smell of wet dog." I glanced at Luna as she trotted beside him, her tongue hanging from the corner of her mouth.

"Just tell Elle it's for the greater good, if she says anything," I told him, imagining the sour look on her face. I glanced at Meghann's house, coming up next, and nudged Beau's shoulder. "Hurry past this one," I whispered, not wanting Meghann to spot us and talk our ear off. I wanted to get to Kat before it got much later.

That was one thing I liked about Kat, she wasn't a talker just for the sake of talking, not overly so, anyway. We could work all day, side by side in comfortable silence, if we wanted to. It wasn't like that with Meghann, who always had some sort of question or comment perched on the edge of her lips.

"Don't you and Kat *always* fight? Why is this time different?" He pointed to the beer bottle in my hand as I quickened my pace.

"Damn, you're full of questions tonight," I realized. I might as well have invited Thea along too. "We bicker, we don't fight. At least, not usually."

"That doesn't mean she needs a gift, does it? If I had to get a gift for Thea every time we fought, she wouldn't be able to close her bedroom door, it would be so full."

"Yeah, well, this is a little bit different," I told him, peering around at the shadows lining the street, in between houses and parked vehicles. I'd snapped at Kat when I knew she'd only been worried, the same as I would've been worried about her had our situations been reversed. It was hard to explain why I had to do what I did for Mrs. Filmore—I just had to if I could, even if it never got any easier.

"Because you like her?" Beau looked up at me. His face was covered with moving shadows as we walked down the sidewalk, the street lamps lighting the road intermittently.

"What?"

"The same way Jackson gets Elle taffy and books and stuff when she's mad at him."

"Oh, well, no. It's not the same as that," I told him. "Now, pay attention to your surroundings. Look for things out of place, or noises that might need looking into."

Beau's eyes darted around to the woods lining the far side of the road and down the cross streets as we passed. I'd only gotten a few moments reprieve when he started up again.

"Do you find a lot of trouble when you go out on patrol?" Beau whispered, and his light brown hair caught in the wind.

"No, not really. I've run into a few people who have had too much of Huck's homebrew," I said, lifting the bottle in my hand, "but they don't want any trouble. This place is a utopia to them, they just want to let their hair down once in a while, and sometimes they get carried away."

"What about Crazies? Do you ever run into any of them?"

"No. At least, not in a long time. The bear, though," I said grumpily, "he's been terrorizing a few of us the past couple of nights."

"He won't hurt anyone," Beau said, but he sounded glum.

"What's going on with you and that animal?" I remembered his argument with Aria at the dinner table. "Why don't you like him, if he wants you to be his human?"

"It's not that I don't like him, he's just a big oaf. He doesn't listen, not like Luna. And he's always getting into trouble. But he's had a connection opened with humans now, it's why he needs one—it's why Luna won't leave my side. We rely on each other for everything. She's another part of me. Aria should be his human. She's the one who brought him around. She's the one who needs a companion, like him. I have one already."

"Then why won't she be his human?"

Beau shrugged and kicked at a rock on the sidewalk, sending it sailing across the street. "She says she's not like me. She connects with a bunch of animals, so she doesn't have a connection with just one. I think Bear needs that, like Luna does."

"But you're at capacity," I realized.

"What?"

I shook my head. "Nothing. Well, poor Bear needs something because he's going to send McGregor into an early grave if he shows up on his doorstep one more time."

Beau sniggered as we made our way up the hill to Kat's. I guess it made sense, that once an animal felt a human connection, it would be hard to go back to normal animal life. Especially for a cub like Bear, who was raised with a connection to both Aria and Beau. Now, neither of them wanted him. It made me a little bit sad for him, the more I thought about it.

As we made our way up Kat's gravel drive, Luna stopped in her tracks and lowered her head.

"Something's wrong," Beau said in a rush. "She smells strangers." I reached my palm out to stop him and surveyed the wooded hillside, seeing the lights on inside Kat's cabin. There was no smoke coming from her chimney, which I would've expected given the storm coming in, but there were no vehicles in the driveway either, other than the Tahoe.

"Does she sense anything else, like how many there might be?"

He shook his head.

"Beau," I said in a harsh whisper. "We're going to approach quietly, okay?" Kat could've had a neighbor over, but as quickly as the thought crossed my mind, I told myself it was better to be safe than sorry. "I don't want them knowing we're here, not until I know what's going on."

He nodded, his eyes wide with apprehension but hardening by the second with determination. Bringing my finger to my lips, I motioned for him to be quiet, and we hurried through the trees, my pistol held down at my side as we moved in haste. I didn't hear anything until I drew close enough to peek in through the living room window, and I clenched my fist tighter around the grip of my gun.

Kat was tied to a dining room chair facing the living room, with blood smeared on her right temple and a gag in her mouth. A young man, about seventeen or eighteen years old pilfered through the boxes in her living room, amusement brightening his gaunt face. He held her pistol in his hand.

This wasn't happening. Not the gangs already—not when we were trying to get ahead of the problem. Silently, I cursed Kat for not taking my warnings more seriously, and then I hated myself for not pressing her harder to listen.

Chest heaving, I squatted down and looked at Beau and Luna, both of them wide-eyed and awaiting direction.

"There's a young man in there, and he's not a friend of hers," I said gravely. "He might be a scout," I thought out loud. I wasn't sure what his Ability was, but it wasn't sensing others or he wouldn't look so pleased with himself, holed up in there with a woman tied to a chair.

"I want you and Luna to sneak around back. Hide in the shadows, but make some noise. I want him to get distracted, and see if I can get him to go outside to take a look. Luna will know what to do if he does." I glanced inside again. The sliding door was partially open, like maybe he'd surprised her by coming in through the back. The boy paced slowly around in the living room, grinning as his lips moved. Kat glared at him in response. I could see the curses churning through her mind, and could imagine what she'd be saying to him if she could.

I looked at Beau again. "It looks like there's only one of them, but I'm not certain. When you go around back, don't engage—do you hear me?" I looked him directly in the eyes. "We don't know what his Ability is, and there may be more of them. Let Luna do the work, she knows how to keep herself safe, and her presence alone will scare the shit out of him while I figure out how to get Kat out. Do you understand? Just distract him."

Beau nodded. "I'll see if there are garbage cans, or something Luna can knock over."

I nodded. "I want that asshole surrounded, but we have to keep the element of surprise. You're not to endanger yourself at any point. That's part of being on patrol, you have to listen to orders."

"Yeah, I will," he said, adamant and a little breathy.

"I'll come in from the front while you've got him distracted."

Unclipping the knife strapped to my thigh, I handed it to Beau. "Just in case," I told him. Beau nodded and gripped the sheathed knife hilt in his hand. "These kids have hurt people, Beau. Be careful, and be smart. Promise me," I urged him, on behalf of me, and Elle, and everyone else who loved him.

"I promise." For all the bravery I saw in Beau's stance, from the hard set of his jaw to the relentless grip he held on the knife, I saw fear in his eyes too, and knew he wouldn't do something reckless. Beau had seen his fair share of bad in the world, and all of us had ensured he would never be helpless.

"You can do this," I reassured him. "Remember, focus on the eyes and nose if it comes down to a fight—find his weak points." With a brusque nod, Beau licked his lips. "Now, go," I whispered, and pointed around the back. "Remember, stay out of sight until you absolutely have to," I rasped, but Beau was already creeping away, and the rustling of his footsteps on the ground was drowned out by the wind as it whipped past.

Once the asshole was distracted, I would go in through the front and surprise the fucker with a headshot if I had to. Either way, he wasn't leaving unscathed.

ELEVEN
KAT

Harlon was his name; the older of the two scouts, pacing around me like a cat playing with its prey. Yet, even with the gleam of intrigue lighting his eyes and his lack of scruples about tying a person up and threatening their life, he was just a kid. A tall, cocky prick of a kid who had never been put in his place, and I was itching to do it.

"Cal, check the cupboards for food," Harlon said, and my eyes shifted to the footsteps I could hear in the kitchen, though I couldn't see the boy he was giving orders to. It was as though the way the light shined on him reflected differently, playing tricks on my eyes, like he wasn't even there. But he was, walking right by me, every footstep told me so.

As Harlon riffled through my boxes, I dreaded what he'd find in the bottom one. "What is all of this crap," he said, tossing my notebook, novels, and JJ's collection of oddly shaped pinecones I couldn't bear to get rid of to the floor. "What are you, a squirrel? Don't you have anything good?"

I rolled my eyes, unable to answer the way I wanted to with my mouth gagged. I growled at him for good measure and tried to stay focused on the task at hand; they'd done a shit job of tying my hands behind me in the chair. I was almost out of my bindings, just a few minutes more was all I needed. Apparently, they'd never tied up a woman before, or if they had, she must not have had small wrists.

"Seriously, I thought we hit pay dirt when we saw that pedestrian bridge down the road. If this is all you people got— preserves and . . . what is it, a kid sketch?" he scoffed at another one of Thea's drawings, and I hoped he continued to bluster and throw a tantrum because it was buying me more time.

Gaze darting into the kitchen, I watched as the cupboards opened and shut. I remembered Cal's profile as it flashed in the moonlight outside before everything went black. He was smaller and younger than Harlon, but I wasn't fooled by his size. He'd been raised a thug, probably by Harlon himself. I wouldn't put it past Cal, even if he was barely in his teens, to do something horrible. I wriggled my wrists slowly, trying not to move my arms and shoulders too much, since that would give me away. I could feel the large rope sliding over my thumb joint.

"Did you just move into this dump?" Harlon said, rising to his feet, and my eyes darted to him. "Where's the rest of your stuff? Where are your weapons? I know you have more." He pointed to my holster, now empty of my pistol and extra magazine.

I mumbled a response because it was all I could do.

"Say what?" Harlon stepped closer, nearly tripping on the notebook he'd discarded, and he yanked the gag from my mouth. "What were you saying, and it better not be a smart-ass comment, or I'll gag you again."

"I said, *yes*. I was just moving in. I don't have any weapons here. I'm a deputy, I don't keep them in my house."

"Where the hell are they then?" he said, shoving the barrel of my own gun into my temple. He pressed it right into the wound that burned and felt cold and wet with blood.

I winced. "At the station." *Just a few more seconds . . .* I wriggled my hands a little bit more.

"Where's the station?" he gritted out. "And feel free to tell me how to get there, while you're at it."

I glared at him, wondering if this of all possible ends was my lot—to get shot by a kid whose balls had just dropped. I hated to think that all I'd been through led to this final moment, even if I wasn't afraid to die.

"Speak up," he growled, and pressed the end of the gun into my temple so hard I screeched. "Or I—"

Something crashed in the wind outside, and Harlon straightened. His yellow-green eyes widened before his features twisted with anger. "You stupid bitch—is someone else here?" He pressed the gun into my head again, but relented and headed to the sliding glass door, more worried about who might be outside than what I could do in here.

"No one else is here," I managed, feeling the fresh blood from the wound he'd reopened dripping down my cheek. "It's probably the wind."

I could hear the rustling of leaves outside, and I could feel the cold breeze coming in from the cracked door behind me. If I was lucky, it was actually Bear this time, though I wasn't sure he would know to do anything.

"Cal, watch her," Harlon ordered, and quietly he slid the sliding glass door open enough to walk through. "If she does anything stupid, shoot her."

Cal flitted into existence in the kitchen again, a bag of what few food items I had in a pile on the counter behind him. A gun was shoved into the waistband of his pants.

I jiggled my wrists as best I could as tears burned the backs of my eyes. I was so close, I just needed . . . a few more . . . seconds.

"What the fuck—" Harlon yowled outside, followed by the snarl of an angry wolf, just as my hands pulled free from their bindings. There was the pop of a gunshot, and while Cal panicked in the kitchen, slowly beginning to register that I was free, I lunged for the bottom box—the one Harlon had been so close to opening—for the other Glock and bullets that were inside.

As my knees hit the ground, the front door flung open and Ross barreled inside.

"Ross!" I shook my head. *He shouldn't be here.*

"Kat—" he said as Harlon's shrieks from the backyard filled the air. Ross reached for my arm before I could warn him.

I saw the shimmer of light play against Cal's profile before the gun in his hands flickered to existence, aimed at the back of Ross's head.

Ross froze and his palms flew up.

"I'll blow your head off if you move!" Cal warned above the snarling and screaming outside. Then suddenly, everything went quiet.

"Don't hurt him," I demanded, but my voice thinned with panic.

Growling resonated behind me, and I heard the clack of wolf claws on the hardwood floor as Luna slunk in. Her bloodstained teeth bared as she stopped beside me and lowered her head in warning.

Cal's eyes shifted from me to somewhere behind me, where I assumed Beau was standing. "Call off your wolf," he bit out, "Or I swear I'll shoot him." Cal inched closer, his thumb worrying the grip of the pistol in his little hand. He knew how to hold a gun, but the uncertainty in his eyes made me think he didn't want to use it, not unless he absolutely had to.

Fight or die. That's what they'd been taught, and I knew Cal wouldn't go down without a fight. Because if he didn't answer to me, he would have to answer to the group he had to go back to.

"You know you don't want to hurt him," I said, and though I tried to sound steady, I was anything but.

Ross's eyes were locked on me, but I refused to meet his gaze. I couldn't bring myself to look anywhere other than at Cal, watching every twitch of his lip and every furtive shift of his gaze.

"Where's Harlon," Cal demanded, though I could hear the slight wobble of his voice. "Where is he!" But Cal knew that Harlon was dead, or he'd wish he were if he still breathed.

"He's outside and probably needs help," I told him. "We can't help him if we're in here." I prayed Beau wouldn't contradict me, because the last thing I wanted Cal to feel was more desperate than he already was.

"He's dead, isn't he?" he said, his dark eyes four sizes bigger with fear. "You killed him, and now I have to go back—do you know what they'll do to me? Do you know—"

"You don't have to go back, kid," Ross said carefully. "You don't have to go back, you can stay here. But if you want to stay here, where it's safe, you have to put the gun down."

Luna snarled and inched closer. "Get that wolf away!" Cal shouted. "Get it away, I'm warning you!"

"Beau," I said without tearing my gaze from Cal; I didn't dare look away, worried what he'd do if I blinked for even a second. "Take Luna outside."

"Do it," Ross conceded, and with a final growl, Luna backed away and retreated to the backyard.

The frightened teen in front of me wasn't a killer—he was a protégé, a young impressionable mind—and I knew if we had a few minutes longer, we could all get out of this alive.

"Where is your group?" I asked him. "Wherever they are, they don't have to know what happened here. You can hide here —you can stay and they will never know."

"They'll come looking," he said, as if my promises of protection and a better life were empty and pointless. "They'll come looking because that's what they do. They hunt you down until you join them, or you die." His voice cracked.

"Just put the gun down," Ross urged, his palms still out in front of him. He was calm and more gathered than I would've thought possible. But it wasn't the first time he'd been held at gunpoint. "We'll figure it out. I'm the law here—we'll keep you safe, just like she said. You don't have to—"

But the instant the kid closed his eyes and shook his head—the moment I realized fear had won out and his finger was moving to the trigger—my mind and body reacted before I realized what I was doing.

Energy crackled in the air around me. The hair on my body stood on end. A hum filled me.

Feeling—not thinking. Sophie's words circled through my head as I reached up and pulled a surge of electricity toward me. With a rush of raw, charged power, a bright, blinding light filled the room, my fingertips burned, and a bolt of lightning broke through the ceiling and right into Cal.

He fell, and with the surge of adrenaline whirring through me and my heart hammering in my chest, I crumpled to my knees too. *Breathe, Kat—just . . . breathe.*

My fingertips dug into the ground as I willed myself to calm down. My limbs felt like limp noodles, spent on a coiling energy I hadn't realized was lying in wait all this time. And as the reality of what I'd done settled in, I looked up and froze with horror. Ross was unconscious beside Cal on the ground, surrounded by smoke.

"Ross," I rasped.

I heard footsteps and heaving breath behind me as Beau ran inside, and I scrambled to my feet. A burn marred the side of his face where the electricity had jumped from Cal's body to his.

"Ross!" I shouted, running over to him. "Ross—wake up, Ross." I fell to my knees beside him. I hovered at first, processing just how bad what I'd done might actually be, then lifted his heavy torso into my arms, frantically feeling his neck for a pulse. "Ross—wake up, Ross."

I'd killed him. He wasn't a Re-gen. He wasn't an experiment. He was a man, and I'd struck him down with a megaton of voltage as if from heaven itself.

I forced myself to calm down and take a deep breath before I lost my wits completely. "Beau!" I choked out, and with trembling fingers, I felt for Ross's pulse again. It was there, just below the surface, but it was weak.

"Beau! Get help—run and get help!" I told him. As certain as I was that Ross had a pulse, I wasn't sure for how long. I glanced back at him.

Beau stood by the door staring, still and horrified with shock.

"Beau! Run!" I cried, and pulled Ross closer into me. He'd come to save me, and I might've killed him instead. "Ross," I pleaded, gripping him tighter. Not like this—I couldn't lose him too, and this time it would undeniably be my fault.

My head shook. "No," I told myself. "No. No. No . . ." It wasn't possible. Ross couldn't be gone; I needed him. And as that realization sank in, tears filled my eyes—the horror no longer keeping them at bay.

TWELVE
ROSS

Kelsey hovered over me, a halo of blonde hair hanging messily around her face, and big, beseeching blue eyes blinked wildly at me. "Ross, can you hear me? Wake up!"

I was awake—confused, but awake.

"Answer me," she demanded. I admired the way her chin trembled when she worried, so open and unguarded, which I rarely saw. "Ross . . ."

It had been so long since I'd seen Kelsey, and there she was, an angel in death, so close I could touch her. I wanted to reach for her but I knew she wasn't real, she'd never be real again, and I found myself drifting further and further to sleep in her warm embrace.

"Ross!" Her voice rang out again, more desperate and imploring, and this time I stirred.

"Ross, open your eyes, God damn it," she commanded. Her warm hands cupped my face, and I felt the dampness of her tears on my cheeks.

Peeling my eyes open, the lines of her blurred face focused. I'd never seen such fear or sadness. It was Kat above me—Kat's golden hair and fear-filled gaze. It was Kat's trembling chin that

I liked so much, and her warm hands against my skin. My chest ached at the sight of her. I didn't want her to worry; I didn't want her to cry. Not for me.

I tried to say Kat's name, but my mouth wouldn't move.

"He's waking up!" she called. I wanted to shush and comfort her, but my mind was too heavy, and my limbs wouldn't move.

There was rustling, and Kat began to back away, hesitant at first, until I could barely see her.

"Kat," I said groggily. I didn't want her to disappear.

Her crumpled face opened, and she rushed closer. "Oh, thank God," she choked out. Gripping my hand in hers, she rested her forehead against it. She muttered something indiscernible as my vision went in and out of focus, then she began to sob.

There was a flurry of bodies and movement, but all I could do was stare at her as my eyelids grew heavier. "Kat . . ." But her name died on my lips, and the world went black.

THIRTEEN
ROSS

Maybe it was exhaustion or the pain meds, but I sat at my kitchen table staring at the wall. There was nothing on it, and it was nothing special, just a beige wall with dust collecting on it. I didn't do much housework. I wasn't home enough to care—until now. Even if I'd been asleep for half of it, the past eighteen hours was the longest I'd ever been stuck within these walls, and it was driving me to the brink of insanity.

I'd never thought of it as a home, just a place to crash and eat. Now that I was cooped up inside, though, I wished it felt like something more than the charging station I'd used it as before. There was nothing worse than being holed up inside, like an invalid in a cardboard box, when all I wanted was to get out of the house; I wanted to know how that damn kid was progressing, if he'd woken yet, and to see how Kat was holding up. I still wasn't certain what exactly the two teens had done to her before I had arrived, and I was wound so tight I thought I might burst out of my skin.

My watch timer buzzed, and I peered down at the blinking reminder. *Afternoon med time. Wonderful.* I pushed away from the kitchen table, ignoring my rumbling stomach. My face and neck felt equally tight with healing flesh as they stung with the deep burn of singed nerves. It wasn't as bad as that, at least not really, but it sure felt like lava had melted the side of my face.

As I made my way down the dark hall, a muffled voice caught my attention from the front of the house, followed by the slamming of a car door. Then I heard Elle's rich alto and knew she was coming to rain hellfire on me after the danger I'd put Beau in last night. And she had every right to. Beau was just a kid, a capable kid, but a kid nonetheless, and we'd been lucky the only casualty, other than my face, was Harlon. I wasn't sure the kid in the coma counted.

I'd been wondering all day how Beau was doing after what he'd seen: Harlon's mauling, Cal pointing a gun to my head, Kat's lightning.

I answered the door as Elle knocked. Her hair was pulled up into a messy bun-thing on her head, and Beau and Luna stood on the stoop beside her. The three of them stared at the gauze covering half of my face.

"It looks worse than it is," I told them, and moved aside for them to come into the house. My gaze flicked around, wishing I'd been more prepared for company, but I realized I didn't have it in me to care too much more than that. Despite my restlessness to get out of the house and be useful, I'd woken feeling more like I was fifty-five, not thirty-five.

Luna trotted in first, sniffing around curiously while Elle and Beau stepped inside, their eyes still fixed on me.

"Ross, are you okay?" Elle asked, her words more of a whisper as she took in the mangled sight of me.

I waved her concern away and was about to nod when I felt my flesh pull beneath the bandage. I tried not to wince, and met Elle's stare. "Look, I know I screwed up last night, and I should never have taken Beau—"

"Ross," she said briskly. "I'm not here to lecture you about last night."

I closed my mouth and straightened. "Oh . . . Well, why the hell not?"

She glanced to Beau, who stood nearly to her shoulder. His blue eyes were wide as he worried his bottom lip. "We wanted to make sure you were all right," she said. "We were worried is all." Again, her gaze shifted to Beau, and I realized how scared he must've been, watching me being carried out of Kat's house unconscious.

"Oh. Well," I clasped Beau on the shoulder, "thanks to those runner's legs of yours, I'm just fine, kid," I told him as easily as I could, and I gestured for them to sit down on the couch. "Can I get you guys some water or something?"

Elle and Beau both shook their heads. "Well," Beau added, "maybe for Luna."

I glanced at her sniffing my scuffed work boots, discarded by the door. "Of course—"

"I'll get it," Elle said, and she gave me an I'll-leave-you-two-alone wink as she stood up and walked into the kitchen.

I could see the concern in Beau's expression, but I wasn't sure if it was because of my ghastly face or if there was something else bothering him.

Elle called Luna into the kitchen, and I sat down beside Beau on the couch, a foot or so between us. "You saved Kat last night, Beau," I told him, and I meant it.

His eyes shot to me.

"I'm serious. I know it was really scary, and really dangerous, but without you and Luna, I don't know what would've happened to Kat."

Beau blinked at me, his eyes filled with both skepticism and hope. "Really?"

"Hell yeah, kid," I said, angling toward him. I bit back the pain as my jaw moved with each word. "You took out a guy a lot bigger than you who had a gun, and he was going to hurt Kat. You did that—you and Luna. You were the ones who ran like the wind to get help while I was unconscious. If you hadn't been there—God, I wish you hadn't had to see all of that—but if you hadn't been, I'm not sure what I would've done. It would've been me and two unpredictable and dangerous gang members while Kat was tied up, and I bet a lot worse would've happened to me than a messed up face. And Kat is okay, because of you." It pained me to say that out loud. That I had let something like that happen to her in the first place was enough to twist my insides, but it was true. "Do you understand what I'm telling you, Beau? You saved us."

The corner of his mouth twitched a little, and for the first time in a long time, I saw him smile with pride.

Like Beau, I'd always strove to have a purpose, so I could feel his satisfaction as if it was my own. I'd always wanted to save everyone when I was younger, to protect my sister from bullies and unruly boyfriends, and the innocent people on our home turf and overseas who couldn't protect themselves—it was why I'd enlisted in the Army to begin with.

An idea formed, and reaching into my shirt collar, I pulled out my dog tag and lifted it over my head. "Do you know what this is?" I asked him.

Beau licked his lips. "Jackson said you got it when you were in the Army."

"That's right, but this isn't just a dog tag, it's more special than that," I explained. "My brothers got me this on my twenty-fifth birthday, they made it for me." I held it out so he could read it.

Beau leaned closer, his lips moving as he read. "Six?"

Once again, I nodded, feeling a sharp spike of pain shooting through my face, and immediately regretted it. "Yep," I said, biting back a curse. "It's what they used to call me."

"Why *Six*?"

"Have you ever heard the phrase, 'I got your six'?"

"Umm . . ." He shook his head. "I don't think so."

"In the Army, it means 'I got your back,' and the guys used to tell me I was the one they could rely on the most, I always had their backs, so they made it for me to remember them by when I was coming back home."

"That's really cool," he said with awe.

"I've always thought so, that's why it's so special to me. Before the Virus, it helped me remember I had brothers who would always be there for me, no matter what—at least the ones that survived." My heart squeezed as I remembered Coleman, who never got to return to his family. "Now, it reminds me there are people here who need looking after more than ever before, and I want to do everything I can to help them." I took in Beau's rapt attention, hanging on my every word, and I knew in that moment that no matter how lost Beau always seemed to feel, he'd be the man he wanted to be—he already was—he just needed to discover it for himself someday.

"More than anything," I continued, "teamwork is what will keep us all safe." I offered him the dog tag, and his brow creased with confusion. "Take it," I told him.

His eyes shot to me. "What?"

"Take it," I repeated.

Tentatively, he did. He stared at the tag in his hand, his mouth pursed in contemplation. "Are you sure you want to give this to me?"

"You're the newest member of the team, Beau. You've more than earned it. Last night you saved my ass, and I know I can count on you, kid."

"Really?" A grin engulfed his face. "Like, *really*?"

Despite the twinge of pain, I grinned back at him. "Of course. I don't know what I would've done without you."

Luna trotted back into the living room, sniffing the stainless steel tag in Beau's hand, then the ball chain hanging through his fingers. Tail wagging and water dripping from her mouth, she licked my hand, draped over my knee, and nuzzled me for a rub behind the ears. With a silent thank you for her help, I obliged and threw in an extra chin scratch for good measure.

"He said I'm part of the team now," Beau said, glancing into the kitchen at Elle. She stood at the kitchen table, arms crossed over her chest as she watched us.

She smiled, excited for him, and maybe a little relieved, then cleared her throat. "An *honorary* member of the team," she clarified. "At least for now." She winked at him, and Beau seemed content with that.

"Of course," I agreed, and nudged Beau. "We gotta train you up a bit, get you warrior-ready, so that Jackson and Elle don't bust my balls too much."

Elle cleared her throat again, glowering at me, and I rumpled Beau's blonde hair as he laughed. "I'm already getting in trouble, this is going to be fun."

Beau chuckled louder with me as Elle walked in and rested her hand on my shoulder. "Can I get you anything while we're here? Make you something to eat, maybe?"

"No, I'm fine," I said. The last thing I wanted was someone waiting on me when I already felt useless. "Unless you can break me out of this prison," I joked. It sure as hell felt like I was locked in one. "Actually, have you heard from Kat?" I asked, anxious curiosity gnawing at me again.

"Not since early this morning when I picked Beau up. She mentioned going to the prison though."

I figured as much. The doc said she'd been with me while I was unconscious, but there were things that needed tending to— an unconscious kid to worry about. I glanced down at my watch again. "I was just about to take my meds when you got here and continue to *rest*, per my orders."

Elle squeezed my shoulder with a soft smile. "We'll let you rest then," she said. "We just wanted to make sure you were okay."

"I'm great now," I said, standing with Beau. "Thanks for

checking on me, bud."

"Sure thing," he said with more pep in his voice than I'd ever heard before.

I clamped my hand on his shoulder and gave him a quick, grateful squeeze, then walked them to the door. With a round of goodbyes and a final pat on Luna's head, Elle, Beau, and the wolf left me to stew again, alone.

Heaving out a breath, I realized I was in some serious need of pain meds, and made my way down the hall to the bathroom. Of course Kat was at the prison. Either she hated Cal and wanted his balls on a spike, or she was worried about how bad off the kid was. Knowing her, it was probably both.

What she'd done to him was as frightening as it was awe-inspiring. I wasn't sure if I felt lucky to be alive, given she had no idea what she was doing, grateful she'd acted at all, or simply stunned that she could do what she did in the first place.

Flipping on the light switch, I stared at my deformed profile in the bathroom mirror. Blue eyes that crinkled with age in the corners blinked back at me. The burns on my jaw and neck were covered by gauze, which I was ordered not to remove until Nathan returned to do it, *"just to be sure they aren't festering."* It hurt like hell, like any burn would, it stung even, but it was the splitting headache that had my mind a little muddled, and the distant ringing in my ears that prevented me from sleeping while I was supposed to be recovering.

I bypassed the willow bark tablets Nathan prescribed, one of Jade's many contributions to the new medical practices White-horse was adopting, and grabbed the bottle of expired Motrin instead. I was a rebel, or so they said. I shook a few pills into my hand and filled the small glass on the sink with water. Unable to tear my gaze away from my gauze-covered face, I chugged the pills down.

Was I supposed to be upset that Kat risked my life or marred my face? Because I wasn't, in fact, the addition might've actually been an improvement. More than anything, I wanted to rub it in her face that she might've practiced a bit more when Elle asked her about it, but I wouldn't. Kat had come through for me, even when she swore she'd never use her Ability again. Even though she hated it.

I startled at the sound of another knock at the door, sending a biting pain through my temple. Maybe it was Nathan—hopefully it was. The gauze on my face was beginning to itch like hell.

Flicking off the bathroom light, I walked back into the living room and toward the front door, my feet moving quickly as I realized it might be Kat. That would be a relief; there were things to say, and I needed to see for myself that she was okay.

There was another knock, and I knew it had to be her, impatient as shit as she always was. "Coming," I grumbled, but when I opened the front door, my anticipation wilted.

Meghann's honey brown eyes widened as she took the sight of me in. "Oh my word, are you okay?"

Meghann was nice enough, but a gossipy, chatty neighbor was the last person I wanted to see.

"I heard it was bad, but—" She waved her words away. "I'm just glad you survived. What a horrible ordeal—and you look so sleep-deprived," she said. "And when was the last time you ate something?" She peered over my shoulder into the house. "Oh, you haven't unpacked? How long have you lived here again?"

I rolled my eyes, wondering how many more times I was going to have to answer that question before people gave up asking.

"Oh never mind, it doesn't matter. Come on, I'll serve you up some of my potato and broccoli casserole." She offered me a dish of food wrapped in a towel as she stepped through the threshold uninvited, still chattering.

Even if her intentions were good, I had to repress a glare and a few choice words. I was going to need something stronger than Motrin if I was going to get through this.

FOURTEEN
KAT

I stood in the doorway of Cal's prison cell, watching his chest rise and fall as he slept. I wasn't sure if he would ever wake up, and even though I knew he was dangerous, what I'd done left a guilt-sized lump in my throat that I couldn't swallow. Cal was just a kid and he might never wake up again. And Ross . . . My chest ached as I considered how close he'd come to death last night. What I could've done differently—all the advice and warnings I should've taken but didn't—were like air horns at a hockey game, blaring in my ears as punishment for being so stubborn and so stupid.

Nathan checked the drip feeding into Cal's arm to ensure he didn't dehydrate during his recuperation, but I was more worried about what would happen if he gained consciousness and somehow slipped out of here, invisible and undetected. Aria, Woody, and Stanley were here, in a different wing of the prison, but still. If no one knew he was coming, he could wreak whatever havoc he wanted.

Cal was just a child in so many ways, and yet what he was capable of, both physically and mentally, was terrifying. He'd been prepared to shoot Ross in the head or shoot me to carry out whatever he'd come to Riverdale to do. I didn't know what the gangs were like, but I could relate to the feeling of entrapment and loss of control. I could understand his desperation to survive.

The markings that feathered down his neck were visible from the doorway of his ten by ten-foot cell, and the previous night came flashing back to life. Me, cowering in shock against the kitchen wall, watching as Sadie and Nathan took Ross away, and Sam and Christine pulling the singed clothing off of Cal's skin. I'd seen the imprint of my power covering his body, the shoots and swirls of scorched flesh, and I was horrified at their beauty.

I stared down at my hands, remembering Sophie's words again. *"It's not about doing and thinking, it's about feeling."* I couldn't sense the charged energy anymore, but I could remember the feeling of it as it surged through me, and the way my fingertips tingled with a raw energy that needed an outlet. If I did nothing, there would always be a chance it would take over one day, or I'd let the hum in the air I sometimes felt seep too far in. Practicing was equally dangerous. And then there was the serum that could fix all of it.

It was pure luck that Ross was still alive, and if I let myself think about it too much, the alternative outcome nearly crippled me.

But he is *alive.* I had to remind myself of that. No matter how dangerous it was to assume I had any control over my Ability, things would've ended much worse if I'd done nothing, and my guilt eased a little.

Woody walked up beside me, a forlorn look on his face that could've been reserved for the child in the hospital bed, or for me. He looked at Nathan as he placed his fingers on Cal's wrist. "How's the patient?" Woody asked quietly.

"Stable," Nathan said, and he glanced up from timing Cal's pulse. "He's strapped down, so whatever might happen when he wakes up, he won't be able to go anywhere."

Woody drew in a long inhale, crossing his arms over his

chest, and leaned against the doorframe. "We've sure got a lot of shit to shovel, don't we." It wasn't a question, but an unpleasant observation.

I looked away from him, my emotions too rampant to answer.

Nathan cleared his throat and grabbed the jacket he'd draped over the stool beside Cal's bed. "I'll be back to check on him later tonight." He glanced one last time at his patient and walked to where we stood in the doorway. "From what I know about electrocution, he should've been awake by now, but then, I'm not entirely sure how much electricity was pumped into him, or what the effects of it will be." His gaze leveled on me as if he was preparing me for the worst.

"Do you think he'll wake up?" My question was only a whisper as I considered this boy remaining a vegetable for the rest of his life.

"I would think so, but it's hard to say. We'll know by the end of today, I think."

Nathan spared a final glance at his patient, then walked out into the hallway. "You should seriously consider moving Stanley and Aria out of here," he said, eyeing Woody this time. "Now that you have an occupant."

"We're already on it, Doc."

"Good. Even though he's strapped down, there's so much we don't know about what he can do or his condition, I wouldn't feel right if you stayed."

Nathan pursed his lips as he looked me up and down. "You need rest, Kat. After last night, you should take a few days to—"

"I can't do that, Nathan." Cal was only one concern of many, and we still needed to figure out where the rest of Cal's friends were, how close they might be, and how many of them we should expect to come looking for him. "There's too much to do, and I—"

"I'll see that she gets some rest," Woody said, squeezing my shoulder. "And maybe some food."

I grabbed my stomach, unable to think about food let alone eat it. "I don't know about that."

"At least try to rest, Kat," Nathan said more softly, his eyes shifting over me.

I ran my hands over my face and through my hair, feeling the exhaustion in my bones.

"Please, for all of our sakes. By the sound of it, we'll need all the manpower we can get soon, so go home and rest."

I couldn't tell Nathan that home wasn't an option, not after what happened there. Not with a part of my roof singed to nothing. Every time I closed my eyes, I saw Ross lying unconscious on my living room floor with a burn down his cheek.

"Woody," Nathan said, handing him his clipboard. "I'll leave this with you for now, for safekeeping. See you tonight."

With a final nod, the doctor was gone, and Woody and I watched the back of him as he headed out of the cellblock door toward the lobby.

"You really should get some sleep," Woody said. "You look like hell."

"I feel like it," I admitted, but it wasn't from lack of sleep or because of the lump on my temple. Daring a quick glance at Woody, I asked, "Have you heard from Ross since this morning?"

His head shifted from side to side, and he studied me closely. "It scares you," he finally said, looking at my hands. "But it shouldn't."

I closed my eyes and took a steady breath. "Of course it scares me. You've seen how dangerous it is."

Woody stretched out his arm and pointed at Cal. "You saved Ross's life because of what you can do. You should never regret that, you should embrace it."

I swallowed, staring into his eyes so full of certainty.

"I heard you talking to Huck about that serum," he said. "I know you're considering it, but I think that's a big mistake."

"You don't know what it feels like—"

"No, I don't, but I know better than anyone what you've been through, and that despite all the experiments and brainwashing, you're like me—finally settled. You have people who need you and care about you here, and you don't know what that damn serum will undo. You don't know how it will change you. Why would you even risk all of that again?"

For the first time, I didn't see Hawk Eyes standing in front of me—I saw Woody. Not the radio voice who my squad thought was crazy for all those years, but the real man behind the voice who had always helped me when I'd needed him most; who had always been so certain and so steady when he needed to be.

Hawk Eyes had been my guiding star in those dark months after the outbreak, the one person I could trust when my own companion didn't even know me; he was the one who got us out of Anchorage when the General's followers began to take over, and he'd trusted me, blindly.

But Woody was the real man. He was the wild eyes behind the voice. The constant presence, no matter how scatterbrained. He was my friend.

"What would you do," he started again, his voice steady and low, "if one of us was in danger again—if you wanted to save Ross's life, but couldn't because you chose to give up the one innate thing inside of you that could help you do that?"

Tears burned my eyes as I imagined the guilt I already felt exponentially, heartbreakingly stronger. Of course I would hate myself if something like that happened, and even if a part of me felt like the weight of my past would dissolve if I didn't have to be reminded of it every time the weather turned, I knew it was selfish. I imagined Cal's gang showing up on our doorstep, unhinged, with Abilities off the charts, like his. Then I thought about my team, who had become my family. What good would I be to Ross—or to any of them for that matter—in the middle of an Ability-charged altercation, if I was no longer superhuman like they were?

"Everything comes with risks," Woody continued. "Especially Abilities like yours, just ask Elle. Let her help you, Kat. Especially before you make a decision like this, because once you do it, it's final."

I stared down at my hands. "I've just decided," I whispered, uncertain why I couldn't see the repercussions sooner. "But I wonder if it might not be a good idea to have some of the serum here anyway." I glanced down the hall of cells. "Just in case we need to use it."

Woody threw his hands up. "That's a whole other ugly conversation," he said.

"But one we have to consider." I met his reluctant gaze. "I know none of us want to contemplate that kind of control, you and I more than anyone, but we need to weigh the options." We didn't know what future awaited us, or if we had to prepare for unrepentant, unbending, dangerous people who could wield powers as great as our own, but we needed to protect the community and the innocent above all else. It was why we started this place and what we'd all worked so hard for.

Woody and I stared at one another for a long-drawn-out moment before he finally conceded. "We'll discuss it."

I nodded, knowing now wasn't the best time, especially when such a grave decision shouldn't be made based on fear, but I also didn't want it to be made out of desperation later.

"Nathan said Ross is home resting," Woody said. "Go see him. Put your mind at ease."

Would it put my mind at ease, or would it make the anxiety worse? I was scared to see the look in Ross's eyes when he saw me on his front stoop. Would he be afraid? Angry? Seething? Would he scold me for pushing against him all the time, because that's what I did—I pushed against Ross so that he wouldn't get too close, and I wouldn't feel for him what I knew brewed beneath the surface. I was afraid to care for someone again, someone who wouldn't love me back—I wasn't sure I could handle it twice. If I went to see him now, I might discover there was more distance between us, or learn that Ross was disappointed in me, and I couldn't stomach the thought.

"Kat?"

I blinked to find Woody's gray-blue eyes shining with sympathy.

"Are you okay in there?" I felt a tear escape my lashes and I brushed it away. With a choked laugh, I nodded. "Yes, fine. I think we both know I could be much worse."

Woody's gaze lingered as he took the sight of me in. "Go on. I promise you'll feel better."

That Woody seemed so certain—scattered-brained, quirky Woody, who never took anything other than conspiracies and his family seriously—made me feel like maybe he was right. I would feel better, and right now, I needed to feel something other than the ache in my heart, and the dread of the unknown. Ross's disappointment or anger would be better than drowning in uncertainty.

Drying my eyes, I smiled. "How is it that you sound like the sane one for once?"

Woody pulled me into him, wrapping his arms tight around me, and the contact felt so foreign, it almost hurt. I couldn't remember the last time someone touched me or consoled me. But that wasn't true. Ross had the day JJ died. It was always Ross—pushing me, testing me, worrying about me.

"The real question is," Woody started, "am I sane, or are you a little bit crazier, like me?"

With a bark of laughter, I squeezed Woody back. "That's a very good question, and I'm afraid of the answer."

FIFTEEN
KAT

Standing on Ross's stoop, I hesitated to knock. Everything might change the moment he opened the door. I stared at his unkempt lawn, overgrown with weeds, and then at the empty neighborhood street lined by houses with innocent inhabitants inside who were now in danger.

I told myself that everything I did to Cal *and* Ross had been necessary to buy us some time and keep everyone safe, even if I'd done a shit job executing it. Ross would want the town to be safe, and I clung to that as I rapped my knuckles against his front door.

There was rustling on the other side, and then voices, which I hadn't expected, before the door opened. I saw Meghann first; her auburn hair pulled half up, wisps hanging prettily in her face. Her hand rested on Ross's forearm, and she looked at me bug-eyed, as if I was an intruder.

I met Ross's equally wide-eyed surprise and I backpedaled. "Sorry, I didn't mean to just drop by—"

"It's fine," Ross said, wincing as he moved his head. "Meghann was just leaving." He looked at her, a silent conversation passing between them, and after a split second, she forced a tight-lipped smile.

"Yes, well . . ." She cleared her throat. "You know where to find me, if you need anything else." Her eyes lingered on Ross a few moments longer, and then she finally stepped past me. Meghann followed the path to the driveway, and then hurried down the sidewalk in the direction of her house, leaving Ross and me alone in the doorway.

With an exhale, I turned to him. "I'm sorry to—"

"Come in," he said, stepping aside, but I couldn't bring myself to look at him. His voice was as reserved as I'd expected, but calm, and I wasn't sure if it was repressed anger I detected or something else.

I stepped hesitantly inside, taking in the boxes and generic setup of his house that I'd seen a hundred times before, uncertain how to start as I felt his presence behind me. I could feel a charge in the air, but it didn't feel Ability-related. It felt foreign and warm. It felt alive.

"Kat," he finally said, when the silence hung too long between us. His voice was a rich hum that felt somehow reassuring, even if it held an edge of whatever was to come.

When I turned to him, his blue eyes meeting mine, he reached his hand out. I stilled as he touched the side of my face. His fingertips brushed the edge of the bandage on my temple, a bit hesitant, then he shook his head, instantly wincing in pain. The raw flesh beneath his bandages was my doing, and a wave of guilt washed over me again.

"How are you?" he asked. "Are you doing okay?"

"Me?" I said, taken aback. His eyes were so soft, and his voice so uncertain, it nearly undid me. "Ross, I'm fine. I—" My chest heaved as I stared at the gauze covering his jaw and neck. "I'm worried about you, not me." I remembered him lying on the floor, his flesh branded with an angry, red wound. If the electricity had burned him even a half inch over, he would be blind, or worse. The tears came in a rush, and I covered my face with my hands. "I could've killed you—"

"Hey," he said, and his fingers wrapped around my wrists. "Kat, I'm fine." He tried to pull my hands from my face. "Look at me—"

I shook my head, tearing my wrists from his grasp, and stepped away from him. "It could've been so much worse."

He took an adamant step closer. "Kat, please," he urged, and grabbed hold of my arms more firmly as he pulled me closer. "Look at me."

Reluctantly, I did, because I couldn't deny him anything— not after I'd scarred his face forever.

"You saved my life," he said in earnest. "I might be dead if it wasn't for you. Don't apologize for that." I could see the urgency in his eyes, wild and gleaming.

But what Ross didn't understand was how close it had really been, and what little control I'd actually had. "You told me to be careful. I thought it was the bear outside, I thought—"

"Shh." He pulled me against him. "None of that matters." His strong arms wrapped protectively around me, and his scruffy face caught in my hair. "I'm just glad you're okay."

"I did everything you told me not to," I sobbed into his chest.

"Kat, if this is the blame game, then I should've built those barricades a lot sooner; it's something I've been thinking about for months."

"If I would've practiced more—if I hadn't decided to move out there, this wouldn't have happened."

Ross's arm tightened around me, and the scent of him—his warmth—enveloped me until I couldn't think straight anymore. Every weakness and every swallowed emotion came bubbling to the surface in a blubbering mess of regrets and apologies.

"Those kids would've come regardless, Kat. If you didn't live out there, they would've gone to Meghann or Christine's house next, and neither of them would've been as prepared." He leaned away, and brushed the damp hair from my face. "*None* of this is on you." His eyes searched mine, like he was willing me to understand, and I did, all too well.

"Then it's not on you, either," I told him. "You can't protect everyone all the time, Ross. I know you think you have to, that you *can*, but this place is too big, and you're only one man—"

"I can protect *you*," he said, his voice a low promise. "And if something would've happened to you when I could've done more, I would never have forgiven myself."

My breath caught in my throat, and I searched the glassy pools of his eyes for meaning. Had I understood him right, or was I looking for an underlying emotion that wasn't there? How long had I yearned for someone to say something like that to me, with so much emotion the weight of it hurt my heart. I hadn't realized how badly I'd wanted it until Ross stared back at me, so sincere and expectant.

"You're not the only one who has regrets," he said, and cleared his throat as he took a step back.

His sudden distance confused me.

"Those kids will likely come looking for Harlon and Cal," he continued. "Stanley was here this morning, and we have a plan. With Alex amplifying Woody, we'll be able to null any other Abilities from getting in. Elle is already out with Jamal getting more weapons, just in case, and Bear and the wolves are on patrol. Aria and Beau are seeing to that."

I sobered as he slipped back into cop mode, and I straightened. "How did you—I thought you were an invalid, and you were in here plotting already?"

"It's what I do," Ross said simply, and he ran his hand over his short hair. "It's what needs to be done, and I won't let something like that happen to you again." Once more, his words felt like a vow, but I was afraid to assume his meaning.

I wiped the tears from my cheeks, unable to look away from him this time. Half his face was covered in bandages, and yet he was still worrying about me. "No one's ever looked out for me the way you do," I whispered, realizing in that moment how true it was. JJ was a beloved companion, but she'd never felt for me what I'd felt for her, and even what I'd felt for JJ, as raw and powerful as it was, didn't feel like this. With her, it felt like an unfulfilled, one-sided and lonely longing. But with Ross, standing in front of me with pain and relief filling his eyes, and determination in his voice, I felt hope.

"Ross . . ." I breathed his name, uncertain what I wanted to say.

His brow furrowed, and he turned and began to pace. "I know no one can ever replace JJ," he said, his voice more tentative than I'd ever heard it before. "And I know we don't get along all the time, but I respect the hell out of you," he said, finally looking at me. "And I care about you. And I—" He stopped in front of me.

Although I hoped I understood what Ross might've been trying to say, and my heart thumped with frenzied joy and relief at the thought of it, I needed to hear him say the words—I needed to know it wasn't only me that felt this feeling. "What are you trying to say?"

His gaze scanned my face, and his jaw ticked as I waited with bated breath. "I think you know," he said, the gruffness thick in his voice again, only this time, it was virile and almost commanding. "I like you, Kat—a helluva lot—and I *want* to be the one who gets to worry about you." His gaze shifted from my eyes to my mouth.

My heart swelled, my vision blurred, and I reached for him. My hand hovered over his bandages at first, not wanting to hurt him, but a part of me craved to touch him. Lightly, I traced the edge of the gauze, feeling the stubble of his jaw and his cheek against my fingertips.

His words filled my chest with a levity I'd never felt before, and the longer his gaze lingered on my mouth, the more deeply his words sank in.

"Well," he said with a clipped breath. "Are you going to say something or just let me stand here like an asshole?" The uncertainty in his eyes belied the roughness of his voice, and I smiled.

Leaning closer, I pressed my mouth to his, softly so as not to hurt him, and felt a curl of warmth unfurl throughout my body. I basked in the feel of his lips against mine, and breathed him in.

It was Ross—the man who had held me in his arms both times I was at my absolute worst; the man who I'd rarely gone a day without seeing in the past three years; the man who pushed against me and challenged me every day, who made me laugh and feel young with every bit of banter. Ross helped give me a purpose here, and he made me feel important. I felt his uncertainty and hope, and I kissed him deeper, like my life depended on it, because in that moment he was everything I wanted, all that I needed, and I couldn't breathe without him.

He wrapped his arms around me with a groan and pulled me closer. Forgoing his pain and all caution, Ross cupped the side of my face and pressed his lips more firmly against mine. They were full and soft, and his palm was rough against the side of my face as a wave of tingles rippled over my skin. Never in my life had I felt so much warmth, and whatever Ross and I were to each other felt right, the most right I'd ever felt. He was the perfect person for me, and I basked in the sensation of it.

After a few heart-stopping moments, he broke our kiss and leaned his forehead against mine. "That was . . . nice," he breathed.

"And all this time, I thought you didn't like my smart mouth."

A grin tugged at his lips and his gaze fell to my kiss-swollen lips again. "It's grown on me," he said with a smirk.

An engine rumbled up the street, and Ross groaned. "That would be Christine and Sam," he said. "I radioed them when

Meghann was here, and told them we had some decisions to make, so she'd leave."

Happy to hear him say that, I leaned in and pressed another kiss to his mouth, not ready to let him go. "Don't worry, Ross," I said against his lips, then I forced myself to pull away. "I'll protect you from Meghann from now on."

He chuckled and brushed my hair from my forehead, his gaze sweeping over my face. "You better." I loved that he was smiling, and I loved that he was smiling because of me.

SIXTEEN
ROSS

Kat and I stood outside Cal's cell, staring in at the boy as he lay there with wide, scared eyes that shifted around the room. All of us had stayed in one room or another in cellblock one at some point. Hell, I even had my very own suite before we began expanding Whitehorse. Now though, it was different. There was a kid inside, a dangerous one who could make himself invisible to the naked eye, something none of us had ever heard of before, Stanley included. But we weren't going to tell him that. This time, the prison was being used for what it was meant for from the very beginning—our protection. I wasn't sure if that was a relief or a looming sign of what was to come.

No society was ever perfect, we knew that going into the rebuilding of Whitehorse, but sentencing or punishing an adult who made life-threatening decisions at the risk of others was a bit more straightforward than a kid doing it. I just hoped that the plan we'd come up with as a group was the right one.

"How many chances do we give him?" Kat whispered, and I'd wondered the same thing.

"He's a kid, and impressionable. You saw how scared he was that Wayland, I think he'd called him, would retaliate. It doesn't sound like he's with them because it's home, but because it's the only option he's had."

"And you think if we give him another option, he'll take it?" She looked at me.

I wanted to shrug. I didn't know much about kids—at least, not about kids these days—but I knew that like anyone else, they wanted to feel accepted and cared about, and we could offer them that if they followed the rules. "I hope so. But it's out of my hands now, the council voted." And if I was honest, it was a relief. My Ability was something I had to bear on my own, but the fate and safety of this town weren't, Kat had helped me realize that. "We just need to lay down the law, is all," I told her. "We need him to know what we expect if he stays."

"We don't have any laws," Kat said with growing amusement.

"Well, I'm going to make some up then."

"You're such a rebel," she said with a smirk, and I loved the way her mouth quirked up just slightly in the corner.

The cellblock entrance opened and Nathan entered with Woody and Stanley. "Hopefully this works," I muttered, and nodded a greeting to the three of them.

"How's he doing?" Nathan asked, drawing closer.

"I think it's safe to say he's shitting himself right about now," I told him. The kid had no idea what was going on or what we were going to do to him. "But he's still tied down, if that's what you're asking. He's still conscious."

Nathan glanced at Woody and Stanley, not as amused as I was by my answer. "I think only Ross, Stanley, and I should be the ones to go in for now. All of us would overwhelm him."

Kat and Woody nodded.

Nathan reached for the doorknob. "Shall we then?" Slowly, he cracked the door open, and Cal's head whipped to the side, his eyes wide and worried.

"Cal," Nathan said, and I stepped in after Stanley so I could leave the door partially open for Woody and Kat to hear.

"What are they doing in here?" The kid's dark eyes were red-rimmed, and I could see the remnants of feathering from the lightning flash on his neck. I was honestly surprised the kid survived, but if Nathan was right, and the kid was telling the truth, it made sense he didn't remember much.

"We came to talk, is all," I told him. "Stanley here runs this place, and is just here to listen." It was partially true. I crossed my arms over my chest and looked into his frantic gaze. "Cal, you said you didn't remember what happened when you first woke up. Do you remember anything now?"

He glanced between the three of us, clearly distrusting. "Not really," he finally said. "I remember the woods, and bits and pieces of a cabin I don't recognize, but then I woke up here."

"You broke into someone's house," I told him, unable to restrain my gruffness as I thought of Kat tied up and bleeding. "And you held a gun to my head."

His eyes widened even more and he swallowed thickly, his eyes shifting from me to the doctor like he'd decided Nathan was his ally here.

"You don't remember where you came from or why you were in a strange house?"

Cal's brow furrowed and he stared at a blank space on the wall as he tried to remember. "I was looking for something—for food."

"Alone?" I asked, testing him.

"I—" Cal shook his head. "No," he said, his gaze darting to me. "I was with Harlon, you did something to Harlon." His chest rose and fell rapidly, and I thought he might have a panic attack.

I prodded a little deeper. "Was he a friend of yours then?"

Cal laughed with fear. "No. He's a bully, but if you have to scout, he's the one you want with you. He's tough. He protects us."

"Who does he protect, Cal?" Nathan asked more gently. "The other kids in the group?"

"Him and another guy, Wayland, have a group, they feed us —we just have to work for them." He clamped his mouth shut. "I'm not supposed to talk about it." He couldn't be more than thirteen years old, which meant he'd been around Beau's age during the outbreak. I couldn't fathom him coming this far without a family to truly care for him.

"Well, kid, you tried to kill me and one of my deputies, so you either talk and tell us what we want to know, or bad things will happen."

"Ross," Nathan chided.

"I swear—" Cal said. "I didn't want to—I wasn't going to shoot you. I just—I didn't know what else to do. I couldn't go back empty-handed. We can *never* go back empty-handed. I didn't know what to do when I heard—" Again, Cal shut his mouth and swallowed thickly. "The wolf," he remembered. "The wolf got him."

I waited for the severity of the situation to sink in, hoping that this good cop, bad cop routine would pay off, even if Nathan didn't realize he and I were playing it.

"Look," I said, widening my stance to settle in for the most pivotal part of the conversation. "I know it's hard out there, Cal, and we want to help you, but you came into our town and you tried to hurt us. What are we supposed to do with that?"

"But I—" He searched for the words, but nothing came. I hoped that meant he didn't want to lie.

"You what?"

Tears clouded his eyes and he shook his head. "I wouldn't have hurt her," he croaked. "At least, I don't think I would have. You just—you don't understand."

I let him simmer for a second as he wiped a rogue tear off his cheek with his shoulder, his arms still bound at his sides. "I'll tell you what I do understand," I said. "Sometimes we don't have good choices to choose from." I thought about Alex and what he'd been through in his life. "I also know that sometimes you get a second chance, so you can start over and make better ones."

With a sniff, Cal looked at me.

"You know why we have you cuffed up, don't you?"

He stared at his wrists tethered to the bed railing, and nodded, shamefaced.

"So, you can see why this is a hard decision for us."

Cal looked from me to Stanley, and then finally to Nathan, who stood silently.

"We're going to offer you a deal."

He licked his lips. "What—what kind of deal?"

"The kind that gives you the second chance I was talking about a minute ago." I sat down on Nathan's stool and rested my elbows on my knees. "You see, we don't have many rules here, but one of them is that everyone deserves a second chance. The problem is, the other rules are about our safety and doing what's best for the community. Now, some might argue that bringing a kid who's done what you have into the community might not be what's best. But then that breaks our second chance rule. Do you see where I'm going with this?"

Cal blinked at me, but I thought he might've looked a little bit hopeful.

"We can't let you go for obvious reasons, so our options are to keep you locked in here, or let you live in our community with us." I let his options sink in. "We don't like violence, Cal—not in Whitehorse. If you decide you want to stay here with us, I have to know I can trust you. So," I said. "Can I trust you, Cal?"

"Yes," he said, his eyes brimming with hope. "You can trust me, I promise."

I glanced back at Mr. Truth Detector himself, Stanley, who was practically smiling with relief, and I had my answer.

"Then here's what happens next," I told him. "You're going to tell me everything we want to know about Wayland and the group, and you're going to stay in here and recover until Nathan says you have a clean bill of health." I could tell Cal didn't like the idea of talking to us about his friends, but that was nonnegotiable. "Are you with me so far?"

Reluctantly, he nodded.

"Then we're going to find a place for you here. You'll have a family to stay with, a roof over your head, and food to eat. You'll have a job, too, and you won't have to hurt anyone or steal anything." I gave him a couple more breaths to let it all sink in, and when the tension in his shoulders lessened slightly, I said, "How does that sound?"

To my surprise, more tears welled in Cal's eyes, and despite himself, his chin trembled.

I cleared my throat. "Then we're good?"

Cal nodded. "Yes, sir."

I didn't have to glance at Stanley; I already knew the kid was telling the truth. I didn't know what he'd been through, but it wasn't something that would be so easily pushed aside or forgotten, and I knew we'd have to be patient with him. "Then I guess that's that," I said, rising to my feet. "Don't try to use your Ability, either. We have ways around that too." I didn't want him to know it was Woody, in case I was off base and the kid was playing me, but I wanted him to know we weren't dumb all the same.

I met Cal's wary but relieved expression one more time, and waited for him to dip his chin in understanding.

Glancing at Nathan, I turned for the door. "Uncuff him before you leave, and make sure he's locked inside." Nathan's eyes widened a smidgen. "Baby steps," I told him. I clamped my hand on his shoulder. "I'll leave you to your patient then, Doc."

As I creaked the door open the rest of the way, Kat was standing in the hall, leaning against the far wall with her arms crossed over her chest. Slowly, she looked up at me with a knowing grin.

I cleared my throat again and continued past her toward Woody's office. "You big softy," Kat whispered in my ear, teasing, and she nudged me with her shoulder. "He had you eating out of the palm of his hand."

I chuckled and shook my head. "Damn kids," I muttered, exhaling the tension from my chest.

"So, boss," she said. "What's next?" Our footsteps echoed down the hall.

"We get on the radio with Hartley Bay and Prince Rupert. We find out what we can from Cal, and get those barricades up right away. We send the scavenging teams out to the immediate areas to patrol until it's done. Then, after we're all safe," I said, thinking about how long that would be, "we figure out what the hell we're going to do about the broods of troublemakers out there."

"Sounds like a good plan, boss."

I quirked an eyebrow at her, relieved there was an easiness between us again, and that she was back to her obnoxious ways. "Can you stop calling me that, especially now?"

Kat shoved her hands in her back pockets with a giant smirk. "Nope, not a chance."

SEVENTEEN
KAT

12 MONTHS LATER

The April afternoon was warm, and I appreciated it, especially on a day like this. There was a roof to finish shingling, and boxes and furniture to be moved. My little abandoned house was livable again, and with the juvenile detention center officially operational, it was time to finally settle down and find a semblance of normality.

Bracing my knees on the newly installed roof, I leaned in and nailed another shingle into place, putting plenty of swing into it. Alex and Sophie, Beau and Thea, and Jackson and Elle had all come to help us move back into the house we'd left untouched and uninhabited while we tended to more pressing matters.

I hammered in another few nails, too excited to see everything so near completion to slow down. With the weather changing, and the roof finally replaced, Ross and I could make a home, something neither of us had had in a very long time.

"You pissed off about something, or just anxious to get back into your house?" Ross asked.

I banged the hammer square on a nailhead with extra force and looked at him with a grin. "Just getting my aggression out, is all." It was a lie, but while many things between Ross and I had changed, my teasing him hadn't.

He scooted a fresh jar of nails closer to me as I made my way down the line. "At the rate you're going, you'll be done by noon, and didn't need all of us here to help you."

"Help *us*," I reminded him. "And yes, we do need everyone's help because I won't stay in that cave of a house you live in another night. A year is plenty long enough."

"It's not like I've had much time to move in," he retorted.

I let my head fall back and I laughed at his same old spiel. "You're totally right. Two years isn't nearly enough time."

"The last nine or ten months don't count. We've been busy as hell and all over the place."

I lifted a conceding eyebrow. "Okay, fine. Getting the barricades up around the city aside, you've had plenty—"

"Are you saying I'm lazy?"

I nearly balked at that. "Like a sloth," I deadpanned, then rolled my eyes. "Of course that's not what I'm saying. I just think it's interesting that you're hell-bent on getting me back in here already, but you've barely unpacked a single box at your place the whole time you lived there."

"Are you two arguing again?" Beau asked from down below.

"No," Ross and I said in unison.

Ross pulled the nail from between his lips and braced his hands on the roof. "It just didn't feel like home. I guess I hadn't found it yet." He winked at me.

"Oh, brother."

Ross leaned in and kissed my temple. "I'm serious," he whispered.

I couldn't help the blush that filled my cheeks, and I allowed a brief moment of contentment.

"Kat," Sophie called up from the truck. She had a box of Ross's things at her feet. "Is this a house box or a shed box?"

"Oh, right inside the door. Thanks!"

"I hope you like the smell of paint," Sophie groused. "Because, thanks to Woody, all of these boxes smell like it."

"Ha. Okay, thanks for the warning." Ross was holding up a shingle when I pivoted back around. "Oh, dear." I straightened. "Is this the last one? Is the roof finally finished?"

Ross chuckled and handed it to me. "Would you like to do the honors?"

"Gladly." I overlapped it with the last row at the apex of the roof, and pulled out a handful of nails. Ross sat back as I went to town on it. One nail in. Two nails in.

"Have you seen the house yet today?" Ross asked over my hammering. "My old room is violet."

"Oh, pretty—Aria's favorite color. I bet you wish you'd thought of that."

"I do, actually."

By the eighth swing, I was grinning like a goon. "Finished!"

There were a few scattered claps below, and Ross gave me a high five. "Now it's time to deal with smelly boxes," Ross said, and he pulled his gloves off by the fingers. We collected our tools and headed down the ladder.

I was happy that Woody and Stanley were finally moving forward with redoing Ross's old house to make it their own. Now that the prison was being used for the rehabilitation program, it was time the trio immersed themselves with the rest of us.

Cal had helped us find Wayland and his crew before they'd found Whitehorse, and we'd teamed up with Prince Rupert to intercede some of the bigger groups we knew were moving too close to home for comfort, even if there were still kinks to work out.

Cal had proven the key to our success, because he was proof that if one of their own could be happy, they could too—they could see the nomadic lifestyle wasn't the only option.

But with more youth, came more safety concerns. We had

nearly four dozen kids in-house, and while most of them were grateful to have a warm place to sleep and food in their bellies, a handful of them preferred the power and independence of life on their own and leading others; for some of them, it was all they knew, and it would take more than our foster program to change that. While many of the youth were glad not to have to move around or follow someone out of fear, there were those who lived for it, and we still had to figure all of that out.

I stopped at the bottom of the ladder and unbuckled my tool belt as Ross descended. "What did the council decide about the serum this morning?" I hadn't wanted to inundate him with questions, since we'd been so busy, but I hadn't stopped thinking about it since the serum had become a viable possibility.

"Since they know it works now, they think we should have some. But, we've decided to bring it to the town meeting and let everyone weigh-in." He glanced over his shoulder at Jackson and Alex, who were fussing with Sophie about something at the back of the truck. "For now, it's a last resort measure—at least, that's what we're hoping everyone will vote on. It's all still very messy, but I refuse to wait for something disastrous to happen to get our asses in gear. We need that serum, just in case."

Like Ross, I worried about the slippery slope of mandating any sort of injection. Stripping someone of their Ability was a safety measure, but nothing was so cut and dry. Those were problems I wanted to leave for another day, though; we had a life of our own to start today.

"Please," Jackson grumbled, and when I looked back at him, he was whispering something in Sophie's ear. She rolled her eyes as he took the box from her.

"What's that about?" I glanced at Ross.

His eyebrows lifted slightly. "Oh, shit," he murmured, and I detected a hint of amusement.

"What?" I glanced at him, but he shook his head.

Alex shifted another box onto the tailgate, telling Sophie to leave it for Jackson as he hurried back for it.

"Oh, shit," I said, echoing Ross's realization.

Sophie glanced up at us as we stood there gaping at her, and she threw her arms up. "Well, I guess the cat's out of the bag now." She tilted her head and glowered between Alex and Jackson.

"Sorry, Soph," Elle said from the doorway. "Jackson's uncontrollable."

Sophie sighed, and her eyes met Alex's as he jumped out of the back of the truck to stand beside her, then they looked out at the rest of us. "We were going to tell you after we were finished moving you guys in, since this is such a big moment for you, but I don't think it can wait that long."

"Sorry, Sophie," Jackson said, scratching his jaw, abashed.

The months and months of hopeful waiting made my heart skip a beat, and I held my breath, waiting for Sophie to confirm my assumption.

"I'm pregnant," she said so quietly, I could barely hear her. "It's been a few months, and I think—I think we're finally in the clear."

"Really?" Thea and I chirped at the same time.

Sophie nodded with a timid grin. "Jackson and Alex are being overly anxious because—well, you get it."

For the first time all day, Alex smiled, as if a weight had finally been lifted, and he stared down at her tummy like an ecstatic, impatient father-to-be.

"I know that's not how you wanted everyone to find out, Soph," Jackson said, but he was too nervous and excited to look overly apologetic. "But . . . I have a really good feeling about it, and I don't want there to be any chance of screwing it up for you." I hadn't seen Jackson that animated in a long time, if ever, actually. He was a jittery mess, more than Sophie or Alex seemed to be.

"It's fine, Jackson," Sophie said, as forgiving as always, and she rubbed his arm reassuringly. "You can give me the rest of that popcorn I know you're hoarding in the pantry in payment though."

Jackson's eyes widened, but he easily conceded. "Wait a minute." He glanced between Sophie and Elle. "You've already been eating it, haven't you? Here I was ready to blame it on Beau or Thea."

Sophie shrugged. "Just thinking about it makes my mouth water, I can't help it." Alex tugged her against him with a laugh and pressed a long kiss to Sophie's lips.

"Gross," Thea and Beau said from the doorway, and Luna trotted out from behind them.

Ross chuckled beside me and shook his head.

"You knew?" I asked him, setting my tool belt on the picnic table.

"No, but I've seen Jackson around pregnant women, and he's a frantic mess."

"I see." I squeezed Ross's hand and headed over to give Sophie a congratulatory hug. "I'm happy for you, Sophie," I whispered, and leaned in to give Alex a hug as well. "You two are going to be great parents."

"Thanks, Kat," he said, his voice a mix of pride, excitement, and hope.

I glowered at Sophie. "Only light duty for you then," I told her, and wagged my finger at Alex. "Make sure she does it."

"I'm working on it," he chuckled. "She's so damn stubborn sometimes—"

"Oh, like you're not?" Sophie countered, and she smacked his arm playfully.

Alex winked at her and took Sophie's hand. "Come on," he said, leading her toward the house. "We'll find you something else to do."

"Oh, I know," she called over her shoulder. "I'll organize your closet, Kat!"

"Have at it," I called back, and she disappeared inside with a contented sigh. I looked at Ross. "Let's get the extra materials into the Tahoe, so that you can drop them back off at the shed when you head to your place for the last of the furniture."

Ross nodded, but his eyes lingered on me for a moment, and his thoughts were somewhere else.

"Uh-oh, your wheels are turning," I realized aloud, and I watched him carefully.

"I was just thinking," he said, a little pensive. "With this rehabilitation project we're getting underway, I think . . . Well, there are going to be a lot of kids who need a home, even if it's only temporary for some."

I felt my heart flutter a little in surprise. "Yes," I said. "They definitely will."

His eyes met mine again, brilliant blue and full of possibility. "We have an extra room. It's just something to keep in mind, is all."

I wasn't sure why his words made me so happy, but my heart felt so full and close to bursting, I almost couldn't stand it. Wrapping my arms around his shoulders, I stared into his contemplative gaze. "I think that's a great idea. And I love you for even suggesting it." His smile reached his eyes, and I kissed him, uncertain how we'd gotten to this moment. Him. We. Us.

"Hello!" A familiar trill met my ears. "Does anyone want some refreshments?" Meghann's voice echoed down the drive, and Ross and I glanced at her and Cal walking toward the house with a cardboard box in each of their arms. "We know you guys are moving in today, and busy-busy, so we brought sandwiches for everyone."

"Oh, Meghann, that's so nice," Elle said, stepping out of the house, and Beau followed after her. He took the box from

Meghann's arms and brought it over to the picnic table, covered in tools.

"Yes, thank you," I said. "This is . . . unexpected." She waved my gratitude away. "Oh, it's nothing. I figured we'd take something to Stanley and Woody since they're moving in today too."

I put the drill back in its box, and the extra nails back into the toolbox, to clear off the table. Jackson, Thea, Alex, and Sophie filed out of the house next, and Meghann looked pleased by the brightness in everyone's eyes.

"We brought quite a variety since I wasn't sure what you all liked." Since becoming the resident chef, it was nice to see that Meghann had finally found something to keep her busy; and motherhood, it seemed, suited her too. I was relieved she had someone new to fuss over now, for her sake.

"Cal, honey, you can set that right there, and let them have their pick." Tentative, he set the box down, his bright blue gaze darting around at everyone. He was familiar enough with all of us, Ross and me especially, and getting more comfortable each day. But he was an outsider, like I had been, and it would take time for him to feel comfortable here, like he belonged.

I stacked the extra shingles against the side of the house. "These look great, Cal. Thank you."

He nodded and shoved his hands in his back pockets.

"The wash bucket's over there," Elle said as she pulled out the sandwiches, each one wrapped in a cloth.

Thea came over to help me clear the rest of the mess off the table. As she reached to move the ladder out of the way, Cal hurried over to help her. While he was older, they were nearly the same height.

"Thanks," she said. They looked at each other with an awkward smile. His hair hung in his eyes; those pretty blues were going to get him in trouble, more than he'd already been in, if I was any judge. Maybe not now, but in a couple of years, Jackson and Elle would have their work cut out for them. Cal was a cutie, and it was only a matter of time before Thea knew it —if she didn't already.

I smiled. There was still a little bit of time for Jackson to warm up to the idea of Thea and any boy being the object of her affection, and vice versa, but I'd have fun watching the process, more than I probably should.

"Will you join us, Meghann?" I asked, nodding to the sandwiches. "It looks like there's plenty."

"Oh, well, sure," she said, nodding at Cal. "Go ahead, honey. Grab one."

Cal looked at Thea. "Do you want a whole or a half?" he asked her.

"Half," Thea said. "Please."

"These are so good," Sophie said, inhaling half of her sandwich in only a few bites. "Is that tomato and cucumber in there? I could eat these all day."

"Good. I'm glad—" Meghann jumped at the growl of a prowling, hungry bear. I could hear Puck whinnying nervously in his paddock, as any animal would in the presence of a grizzly. "Puck is never going to get used to that," I grumbled.

"*I'm* never going to get used to it," Meghann muttered.

Bear lumbered through the trees and closer to the house, all three hundred pounds of him. He was massive and still a bit unruly, but he was still harmless.

He lifted his nose to the air, sniffing out our feast, and I looked at Beau.

"Yeah, yeah," he said. "I'll get rid of him."

The bear chuffed and peered around at us, his eyes finally locking on Beau as he climbed off the bench. "Here," I said, handing him a couple of sandwiches with a wink "Don't be too hard on the big guy."

Beau took the sandwiches, told Luna to stay, and headed over to Bear, reluctant.

Bear might not have been what Luna was to Beau, but he was important to all of us. He helped patrol the borders and kept us safe when he was around, which was more than Prince Rupert could boast. He pulled his weight, even if there was a lot of it, and even he needed a little bit of love.

Ross snaked his arm around my waist and handed me a sandwich as we watched Beau stop in front of Bear, who nudged him happily. Beau reached out and scratched the top of Bear's head, then put the first sandwich in the grizzly's mouth, waiting for him to swallow it. A second later, Beau fed him the other. When he was finished, Bear sat on his back legs with a grumble and pushed at Beau's shoulder playfully. Whatever Beau's hesitation was to connect with the grizzly, it was clearly one-sided.

"That bear will never leave him," Sophie said from the table behind me. I glanced at her as she licked her lips, watching them together. "One day, Beau will be grateful for it too."

THE END

I hope you enjoyed Kat and Ross's story! Fast forward a few years and find out what happens next in Beau and Bear's adventure, *Untamed*!

Series audiobooks, ebooks, signed paperbacks, and book bundle discounts are available in my bookshop.

You can find more information about membership exclusives, newsletter signups, and more on my website:

www.lindseypogue.com

OTHER BOOKS BY LINDSEY

FORGOTTEN WORLD

(Stand-alones, suggested reading order)

RUINED LANDS

City of Ruin

Sea of Storms

Land of Fury

FORGOTTEN LANDS

Dust and Shadow

Borne of Sand and Scorn Prequel Novella

Earth and Ember

Tide and Tempest

THE ENDING WORLD

SAVAGE NORTH CHRONICLES

(Reading order)

The Darkest Winter

The Longest Night

Midnight Sun

Fading Shadows

Untamed

Unbroken

Day Zero: Beginnings

For behind-the-scene access to exclusive projects, check out my VIP reader community.

ABOUT LINDSEY POGUE

Lindsey Pogue is a genre-bending fiction author, best known for her soul-stirring survival adventures and timeless love stories. As an avid romance reader with a master's in history and culture, Lindsey's series cross genres and push boundaries, weaving together  facts, fantasy, and romance set in rich, sweeping landscapes of epic proportions. When she's not chatting with readers, plotting her next storyline, or dreaming up new, brooding characters, Lindsey's generally wrapped in blankets watching her favorite action flicks with her own leading man. They live in Northern California with their rescue cats, Beast and little Blue.

For newsletter signups, memberships, exclusive content, and bookshop discounts, visit the Savage North Hub.

www.ingramcontent.com/pod-product-compliance
Lightning Source LLC
Chambersburg PA
CBHW051458050726
47593CB00005B/2124